THE RUNAWAY

THE RUNAWAY

Alistair Brown

CHRISTIAN FOCUS PUBLICATIONS

© 1994 Alistair Brown
ISBN 1-85792-101-1
reprinted 1999

Published by Christian Focus Publications Ltd.
Geanies House, Fearn, Tain, Ross-shire,
IV20 1TW, Scotland, Great Britain
www.christianfocus.com

Cover design by Donna Macleod
Cover illustration by David Dowland
Reproduced with kind permission of
David Lewis Illustration Agency.

Printed and bound in Great Britain by
Cox & Wyman Ltd, Reading, Bucks.

Contents

CHAPTER 1

Wendy screamed in terror as the knife blade flashed only an inch from her face. She ducked and weaved from side to side, trying to get away from the dark stranger who was attacking her.

Desperately she looked for some way of escape or a place to hide, but she was trapped down a blind alley, her way barred by a brick wall.

"I'm going to kill you!" the evil assailant murmured quietly, moving slowly in Wendy's direction.

"Help! Somebody help!" she screamed, fear written all over her face. But no-one heard. She was alone with a madman.

He stumbled forwards, reaching to grasp her arm, his hand clutching the knife which would drive the life from her body. Wendy's back was to the wall. There was nowhere else to run.

Her mind raced. There was just one chance...

Her knee shot up, butting heavily into her attacker's stomach. He let out an enormous roar and clutched his middle. It gave Wendy the second she needed. She crouched low and darted straight through the man's legs. Now she had to run for her life.

She summoned every ounce of strength to make her dash for freedom. She sensed the man with the knife turning to catch her again. Her feet pushed hard as she sprinted away. This was her only hope.

What she didn't see was the refuse can tipped over at the side of the alley. She had taken no more than six strides when she ran straight into it, falling head over heels. She landed heavily, the breath knocked from her body.

Before she could pick herself up and run again, the knife man was on her, pinning her to the ground. Wendy twisted round, and saw the knife lifted high to strike. Her hand shot out, grabbed the attacker's wrist, and held the knife away. Survival now depended on winning a battle of strength.

Wendy's face contorted with the effort of resisting the downward pressure of that menacing arm. But it was hopeless. What chance did a fifteen-year-old have against an adult? Slowly her energy was going. Inch by inch that knife was getting closer to her face.

At most Wendy had seconds to live...

Lights blazed, and a voice shouted, "Well done Wendy and Fred. That was great acting. It's at that point our hero comes along and rescues you, but we'll rehearse that part another time. Good! This school play is going to be the best yet." It was Miss Roberts who spoke, English teacher, and leader of the school drama club.

Fred gave Wendy a helping hand up from the stage floor. "Thank you," she said, dusting herself down. "I'm glad you're not a real villain. I'd be pretty frightened of you," she added with a smile.

Her fellow actor laughed. "I'm harmless really."

So he was. Fred was in final year, and one of the gentle giants of the school. There were very few who seemed to be liked and respected by all the pupils, but

Fred was one of them. "See you at the next rehearsal," he called after Wendy as they took different directions.

"Bye!" she shouted back, and hurried into a nearby classroom to change out of the old jeans she'd worn for the rehearsal, and put on something a little smarter for the walk home. Wendy was always concerned about her image. "You never know who you might meet," she would say to those who teased her.

It took only one minute to change, and another five to straighten her hair. She picked up her rucksack, and headed for the main exit from the school.

"Hi!" she called, as she saw a familiar figure standing near the door. "Were you waiting for me?"

"As usual..." came the weary reply, but from a face which was smiling. Helen Shaw was best friends with Wendy Jones, and quite familiar with passing time until her more erratic companion turned up. "Did you have a good rehearsal?"

"Brilliant!" Wendy enthused.

"I'd like to have sat in and watched it, but there was a 'No entry' sign on the door into the hall."

"You mustn't spy on us," Wendy warned with mock seriousness. "The play has a great storyline, and it would spoil the performance on the night if the audience knew what was going to happen next."

"Sounds mysterious," said Helen, turning for the door.

"It'll scare most people to death," Wendy grinned enthusiastically. "I'm going to really enjoy it." They walked across the playground, and set off down the road from school.

Helen smiled. "It's funny how we're friends, and yet so different. I mean, nothing would persuade me to get

9

up on a stage in front of a crowd of people. Yet you love it. Don't you get nervous?"

"A little," Wendy admitted, "but I almost like that as well. It's a challenge."

"One I can do without, thank you."

"Maybe it's good we're not the same. That way we're always talking about different things and we don't get bored with each other."

"What have you got planned for tonight?"

"Not much, I suppose. There are two TV programmes I must see, and Dad could bring home a video for us to watch. Then," Wendy laughed, "if there's spare time I might manage to do my homework for school."

"I'm never quite sure if I should believe you when you say things like that," said Helen. "My Mum and Dad tell me I have to do schoolwork first, and other things happen only if there's time after that."

"In that case you need a course in parent management," chuckled Wendy. "Plus a TV in your bedroom, so they don't know when you're watching instead of working."

"There's no chance of a TV of my own. Sometimes we seem to have so little money I'm grateful we have even one television in the house."

The thought of only one TV, and no guarantee of seeing programmes without your parents around, appalled Wendy. She liked independence in matters like that.

Her father earned high wages, and buying things for the house never seemed to be a problem. As well as her own TV, Wendy had an expensive stereo system in her room, plus hopes for her own video recorder for Christmas. Her long term ambition was a private phone, so she could call her friends when she liked, and for as long as she liked.

By now the girls had walked to the point where their routes home separated. Helen lived just on the edge of town, and she had to turn back up a different road. Wendy's house was a large villa set on the main road near the town centre.

"Give me a phone call later if you're bored," Wendy said as they parted. She teased, "I'm sure I could squeeze in five minutes for you between all the other things I have to do."

"That's certainly kind of you, your majesty," replied Helen with a pretend bow. "Bye! See you tomorrow!"

"Bye!" Wendy called back. She hitched her rucksack higher on her shoulder, and headed home. It had been a great day, with a pleasant evening to come. Wendy felt good.

* * * * *

Something was wrong. Wendy wandered through the hall, and headed towards the kitchen. Why had there not been the familiar cheery "Hello!" from her Mum when she came through the door? Why was her Dad's car parked in the drive outside? He wasn't usually home at this time of day.

She edged open the kitchen door. "Hi Mum, Dad..." she began, but the words withered on her lips.

Her mother sat at the kitchen table, head resting on her hands, not glancing up as she entered the room. Her father was leaning against a work surface, staring into space. The silence was terrible.

A strange, unsettling feeling crept over Wendy. The rucksack slid from her shoulder, and she let it drop to the floor. For a second her mother looked up. Tears stained her face.

"What's the matter?" Wendy asked in a quiet voice. "Has someone died?"

"Ask your father," said her Mum, with a harsh edge to her voice that her daughter had not heard often.

Wendy threw an anxious look at her father, but he stayed still, not saying a word.

"Well? Tell her!" her Mum barked.

Mr Jones shifted his weight from one foot to the other. Wendy walked over to him. "What is it?" she quizzed, staring into his distant eyes.

He glanced down nervously. "There are some things which are difficult to explain to a fifteen-year-old..."

"Difficult to explain to anyone!" interrupted her mother.

Mr Jones sighed. "I haven't got any correct words to say this, but..." He hesitated.

"But what?" asked Wendy, not knowing what he would say but fearing something dreadful was about to come.

"Well, your Mum and I can't live together any more."

Her brain whirled with confusion. What was he saying? "Do you mean you have to go away for a while to work somewhere else?"

"No," he replied. "We've not being getting on together very well for the last while, so we've decided to separate."

Mrs Jones began to sob loudly. "You mean *you've* decided. I didn't bring this about."

Wendy didn't know whether to turn to her, or try to get clear in her mind what her father was saying. "I don't understand," she cried out, exasperated and confused.

Her Mum pulled a tissue from an already half empty box, wiped her eyes, and said, "What your father is *not* telling you, is that he's found himself a girlfriend and he's going to stay with her from now on."

"What?" stammered Wendy. "A *girlfriend*?"

"She's just a friend. I'll explain better another time," her father said hurriedly.

"Well, whatever she is, your Dad is leaving us and going off to live with her."

"No!" Wendy screamed. "No! That can't be true."

"It *is* true," Mr Jones said quietly.

"I won't let it happen," Wendy retorted.

"Try stopping him," her mother said harshly. "He won't listen to me. Besides, I'm not sure I want him any more."

Wendy's head reeled. Was she dreaming? Maybe she was having a nightmare, and any moment she'd waken up. She'd walk through her door in the real world, and her Mum would be making the evening meal as usual, with her Dad due to drive home an hour or two later. The sound of her mother's crying broke into her thoughts. This was no dream, but a terrible reality. These were her parents, her Mum and Dad, and they were splitting up.

Deep in her stomach Wendy felt sick. Every part of her wanted to disbelieve what she was seeing and hearing, but her eyes and her ears were sending a different message. Her safe, comfortable world was crumbling. Suddenly anger exploded. She shouted, "I hate this! I hate this! You can't split up! It's not right! It's not fair."

Her father reached out to hold Wendy, but she shrugged his hand away, spun on her heel, and ran for her bedroom. She slammed the door behind her, flung herself on her bed, and cried and cried and cried.

* * * * *

13

The doorbell rang loudly. Wendy glanced over at the clock on her bedroom wall. It was a little after six o'clock.

From downstairs her mother's voice called, "Wendy! It's Helen!"

"Thanks, send her up." Wendy pulled a tissue from its box, dried her eyes, and then consigned it to the bin along with the 30 other soggy remnants she'd used in the last two hours.

"Hello," Helen said gently, creeping round the door. "Are you alright?"

Wendy said nothing, but tried to force a smile in her friend's direction. She was sitting on the floor in the corner of her room, and made no effort to get up. Helen closed the door, pulled off her coat, and tossed it on the bed. She crouched down beside her, put an arm on her shoulder, and looked at her tear-stained face. "How are you?" she asked gently. Wendy shrugged, and said nothing.

All Helen knew was that something terrible had happened. Wendy had phoned her an hour before, but had made little sense since she couldn't stop crying. Helen heard her say that everything had gone wrong, and nothing would ever be the same again. But there were no details.

"I'm sorry I couldn't get here sooner, but Mum made me eat my meal first. Then Dad brought me round in the car, and he'll collect me again in a couple of hours." Wendy nodded, grateful Helen had come.

"Thanks for being here," she stammered.

"That's no problem. When I told my Mum and Dad how you sounded, even they said homework could wait."

A deep silence fell. Helen squatted down on the floor,

14

leaning against the wall. She knew Wendy would open up when she was ready. Her friend stared blankly straight ahead, her eyes lacking their usual sparkle. It wasn't like her to be so quiet. 'What could have happened?' Helen wondered. Had there been an accident? Was Wendy ill? Were her family moving home?

"It's Dad," Wendy said suddenly. "He's going."

"Going?"

"Leaving us. He's going to stay with someone else."

Helen tried to make sense of her friend's words. "Why is he doing that?" she asked cautiously.

Wendy's voice became hard. "Mum says he's got a girlfriend, and he's going to live with her."

"Oh..." said Helen. She nodded quietly, though inside her mind the thoughts were racing. Of course some men walked out on their marriages - some women too - but Mr Jones? Not Wendy's father? Helen sat still beside Wendy, each choosing silence again since there was nothing else to say for the moment.

After a few minutes, Wendy pushed herself to her feet. "I'll put on some music." She picked out a CD, and slotted it into the player her Dad had bought her for Christmas. She'd been so thrilled when she unwrapped the huge parcel. What a great father he'd seemed then, spending so much on her. He was always doing things like that. But now she'd give back every present she'd ever had from him if only she could change the news of the last two hours.

Once the disc was playing, she turned back to her friend. "I'll get us some Coke to drink, and then I'll tell you the rest I know. But it's not much."

"Thanks, I want to hear," Helen replied, as Wendy slipped out the door.

15

A little later, Coke can in hand, Wendy began a moment by moment account of coming home, finding her father there, and everything that was said. At points she struggled to speak, and Helen could see how much this hurt. Sometimes Wendy stopped because she couldn't say the words, or the sobbing became too much for her. But finally it was all out.

"It seems fairly well decided in advance by your Dad," said Helen.

"Yes. I think he'd made all his plans, and then came home early today to tell Mum."

"When is he going?"

"He's staying tonight. Mum says he'll have to sleep in the guest room! But he's packing up a lot of his things right now, and he's leaving in the morning."

"When will he come back?"

"I don't know..." she began, but the dam of tears burst completely at that moment and she couldn't go on for crying. A frail, hurt Wendy shook as waves of sobbing poured over her. Helen put down her can, pulled her friend close, and hung on to her. She had no words to say to take away the pain. She felt helpless to make any difference to what was happening to her friend's life. But she cared.

After a while Wendy calmed down, and sat up straight. But when she spoke there was anger in her voice. "Everything was so good for us. We had all we wanted. Why does he have to do this?"

"He doesn't mean to hurt you."

"All he's doing is thinking of himself. He doesn't care about Mum, and he doesn't care about me."

"I'm sure that's not true, Wendy."

"Yes it is. If he cared, he wouldn't leave. I hate him."

16

"You don't mean that."

"Yes I do. And I won't be saying 'Good-bye' to him in the morning. If he's leaving, he can leave without seeing me."

Helen decided to try one more way to help. She was normally fairly quiet about her Christian faith, but if ever Wendy needed God's strength it was now. "Could I say a prayer for you, and for your Mum and Dad?" she asked.

"A prayer!?" Wendy got really angry. "A prayer? I don't want to hear a prayer. What has God got to do with this?"

"Well," Helen said defensively, "he can make things change."

"If he can make things change, he could have stopped them happening in the first place. But he didn't, did he? So don't talk to me about God. He doesn't care either."

With that, Wendy began to cry again. Helen put her arms round her friend, letting Wendy's tears fall on her shoulder. It seemed a hug was the only thing she could do for her.

* * * * *

Helen hadn't been surprised when Wendy wasn't waiting at their usual corner the next morning. She was bound to take a day off school after being so devastated by her Dad's news.

Mr Jones would leave that morning. As she wandered up the road towards school, Helen wondered what it must be like for Wendy to have her father walk out for the final time. Despite what she'd said, Helen was sure Wendy was bound to see him go. But what would they say to each other? Would she give him a hug and a kiss before

17

he went, like she usually did when he set off on a business trip? Would she stand in the front driveway and wave good-bye? Helen wanted to cry just thinking about it.

The morning passed slowly. Helen's heart wasn't in that day's subjects, and she longed for classes to be over. Finally the bell rang to signal lunch-time, and Helen headed for a phone booth.

"Hello, Mrs Jones," she said when her call was answered. "This is Helen. I'm phoning to ask how Wendy is feeling today."

"Helen..." Mrs Jones' voice sounded hesitant. "I don't really understand. You should know better than I do at this precise moment. I haven't seen her since she left for school at the usual time."

Now it was Helen's turn to hesitate. After a moment she said, "Mrs Jones, Wendy wasn't waiting for me today, and she hasn't been in any of our classes this morning."

"She must be there. She left with all her school books. In fact, her rucksack was even larger than usual..." Mrs Jones' voice trailed off. A terrible thought had crossed her mind. "Hold on. I'm going to check on something." Helen heard the phone being dropped, and the sound of feet running up the stairs.

Within two minutes, the phone was picked up again. "Helen, I've found all of Wendy's school materials shoved under the bed. I've checked her wardrobe. Some of her clothes seem to be missing. That's what she must have had in her rucksack when she left here."

Mrs Jones was speaking quickly, and Helen was struggling to grasp the significance of what she was saying. "I don't understand. What does that mean?"

"It means she's gone..."

"Gone where?"

"I don't know. She's just gone. Run away!"

The phone fell to the ground again, and all Helen could hear was the terrible sound of Mrs Jones crying.

CHAPTER 2

Wendy trudged the streets, not sure where to go. She'd left home that morning, her rucksack over her shoulder with a few clothes, but with no clear plan of what she should do.

If she was uncertain which way to take, she was very certain she couldn't simply carry on with life as if nothing had happened. Her world had fallen apart. From the earliest she could remember there had been Dad, Mum and her. If she had something exciting to tell, they were there to listen. If some problem bothered her, they were concerned. If she hurt herself, they picked her up, held her, and made everything seem so much better. Sure, she liked her personal TV, her expensive clothes, the CD player, and the holidays they took in up-market hotels. But none of those mattered in the slightest compared to having her Dad and Mum with her. Now one of them was gone. Life could never be the same again.

A slight rain began to fall, and Wendy pulled the collar of her jacket a little higher to keep out the cold. She shivered. She'd been walking around for several hours now, and the chill had crept into her bones. To make it worse, her legs ached. Exercise had never been high on her list of priorities.

Knowing she couldn't keep walking forever, and with

her stomach protesting that it was hungry, Wendy turned into the door of a small cafe in a side street. She laid her rucksack and jacket on a chair, and sank wearily into another. It felt good to sit down.

"Hello there, what can I get you?" came a cheery voice. Wendy looked up, startled but instantly taking charge of herself. The question came from a young man wearing a long and partially white apron. He was slim, fairish hair, about twenty, and Wendy reckoned he was good looking, apart from the apron. "You seem rather worn out, my friend. I reckon you deserve at least three courses from our menu," he said brightly.

Wendy smiled, picking up the rather tattered piece of card from the table which was flattered to be called a menu. She ran her eyes quickly down the list: burgers, sausages, pizza, sandwiches, pies. 'Not exactly home cooking,' she thought. "Maybe I'll have a burger and a cup of tea," she said.

"OK, one burger and tea coming up." The fellow disappeared behind the counter, and Wendy looked around the cafe. Although she'd stayed in the one town all her life, she'd never been there before. "It's not our kind of place," her father would have said, and moved them on to a hotel or high class restaurant.

The walls looked long overdue a coat of paint, but the worst patches were covered by posters ripped from magazines. At most there were only a dozen tables in the cafe, none of them with a table cloth. Instead each had a small vase of flowers. Wendy reached forward to catch the fragrance of the flowers on her table, before realising that would be difficult since they were made of cheap plastic.

She was the only customer, and sank back in the seat

and closed her eyes. She felt so tired. She'd tried to sleep last night, and nearly managed it several times. But whenever her eyes had closed, her brain had seemed to switch back into gear, with some new and terrible thought about her Dad leaving, and then she'd been wide awake again. But now, after walking the streets and racking her brains about what to do, she was really exhausted. She could go to sleep right there...

"Burger and tea for the young lady!" came the voice. Wendy jumped up, embarrassed that she'd been caught not paying attention. But the waiter smiled warmly, and her embarrassment was instantly replaced with a much more pleasant feeling.

"Thanks, that's great," she said awkwardly, as he laid down a plate with her burger and a mug of tea. "How much do I owe you?"

"We'll talk about that in a minute," he said, slouching down into a seat beside her. "So, why are you not at school today? Taking some time off...?"

Wendy was caught out by his question. She hesitated before mumbling, "I don't have any lessons today."

"Oh, really?" He sounded unconvinced.

"Yes, this is an out-of-school day for me," Wendy went on, her voice becoming stronger. She wasn't an actress for nothing. "I have other projects to tackle." She didn't like lying, but, she convinced herself, what she was telling him was true...in a way. She did have bigger projects to face, even though they had nothing at all to do with school.

"So, tell me about yourself," invited the young man.

Wendy sipped her tea, taking a moment to think about whether she wanted this conversation. Another glance at the rather handsome fellow persuaded her she did. Besides, a little warmth was gradually coming back into her system, reviving her outgoing nature.

"I'm Wendy," she said. "What's your name?"

"Bill - Bill Smithers at your service," came the reply. "And I'm pleased to meet you Wendy."

"What do you do around here then?"

"Just about everything," said Bill. "I'm the manager."

That sounded important, but Wendy was not that easily impressed. "Who do you manage?"

The question caught Bill out. "Well, it's not so much 'who?' as 'what?' I manage the cooking, the serving, and the clearing up."

"So you're the only one who works here?"

"I suppose you could say that," Bill replied grudgingly. He wasn't used to being on the defensive to anyone, far less to a young female customer. "Hey, I was asking the questions!"

"Don't worry about it," said Wendy, anxious to keep the attention away from herself for the moment. "How long have you been here for?"

"I came a few months ago, got the job and a place to stay a couple of streets away. It's not too bad."

"Why did you come?" Wendy persisted, managing to take a bite at her burger between questions.

"Things weren't working out where I was before," Bill replied vaguely, turning his eyes away from Wendy as he spoke.

Wendy sensed his discomfort, but something inside made her want to find out exactly what he meant. "What do you mean that 'things weren't working out'?"

Bill stared into space. Wendy wasn't sure if he had heard her question, but she waited for an answer with unusual patience. The silence was intense. Finally Bill turned back to her. "There wasn't a lot of happiness back home. Then my parents split up. I couldn't cope with it, so I cleared out. I moved around for a time, and now here I am."

Wendy nodded, with a level of understanding and sympathy she could never have had before. For a while she didn't trust herself to say anything. Bill was looking away again, perhaps reliving some painful memories she reckoned. She concentrated on her burger and tea, glad to fill the empty space in her stomach.

"Maybe home life hasn't been so good for you either just recently," Bill said suddenly. Wendy nearly dropped her mug with surprise. 'How did he know that?' Although her question wasn't spoken, Bill sensed it. "Don't stare at me as if I'm from the Secret Service," he laughed. "It wasn't so hard to guess. You come in here looking tired and miserable, give me a story about not needing to be at school, then go out of your way to avoid talking about yourself. I don't need to be a mind-reader to know something's wrong."

Wendy hung her head. A moment later giant tears were rolling down her cheeks. She sniffed, but found a large handkerchief pressed gently into her hand. "It's okay," said Bill. "Wipe your eyes, and I'll get you another mug of tea."

"Thanks," Wendy murmured. She felt awkward, but at least here was someone who cared. Within a couple of minutes he was back sitting beside her, and this time it was Wendy doing the talking about herself. Everything that had happened since the previous afternoon came out. Bill listened, nodding quietly. He said almost nothing, only once or twice interrupting to make sure he'd understood the torrent of words flowing from Wendy.

"Thanks for telling me," he said softly when Wendy finally stopped.

"Thanks for listening," Wendy smiled through eyes still wet with tears.

"Where are you going now?"

"I don't know," Wendy said. "I just set off because I couldn't stand being at home without Dad. I guess I'll find somewhere."

"That might be hard. There aren't too many places you can go. Almost none at all that I can think of."

Deep inside Wendy knew he was right. She'd been shutting out the hard question about what she would do when night came. She wasn't even sure she could keep walking around for much longer. Bill seemed a kind person. "Have you any ideas?" she asked.

"Maybe..." He smiled at her warmly. "There's a bit of space where I'm staying. You could come there, just until things settle down."

Wendy felt a sudden chill of fear. Ever since she'd been old enough to understand anything, she'd heard warning after warning about not speaking to strangers. Her parents had told her, and so had teachers. Occasionally policemen had come to the school and they had said children should run away from anyone who suggested they go with them. But now here she was, with nowhere to spend the night... 'I'm not a little child any more. I'm fifteen and I can look after myself. It would be okay.' But... She wasn't sure. It was hard to set aside everything she'd been told.

"Thanks for the offer, but I don't know yet," she said in a strained voice. "I'll need to think about it, and see what other possibilities there are."

"But we've already agreed that there aren't any other

possibilities," Bill persisted. "There's nothing for you to worry about. I only want to make sure you're safe."

That sounded so good to Wendy. Bill was obviously different from the kind of people she'd been warned about. Hadn't he been really gentle, and helped her when she was upset? Yet, she didn't know him and her inner fear wasn't going away. She couldn't simply ignore it.

"I'm not sure," Wendy said, getting up to go.

"Well, if you want to take up the offer, all you need to do is be back here by the time I close up the cafe. That's about 7 o'clock."

"Okay, thanks." Wendy opened the door to leave, then remembered she hadn't paid. She fumbled in her pocket for money.

"Forget the cost, Wendy. I'll cover it. It's been a real pleasure to meet you." Bill smiled, and Wendy knew he meant it.

"Thanks. Thanks for everything." She turned away, but as she went out the door she looked back over her shoulder. "Maybe I'll see you later," she said quietly.

"I hope so, Wendy. I've got just the place for you."

* * * * *

"I don't know where else to try. I've phoned Wendy's father, and everyone else who might have some clue where she'd go. So far, no-one knows anything." Mrs Jones was bringing Helen up to date with the news as they sat together at her kitchen table, sharing a pot of tea.

Helen had gone straight to Wendy's home after school. She'd wished she could have taken the whole afternoon off to look for her friend, but school regulations didn't allow absence just because a fellow pupil had failed to turn up for classes.

"Have you no idea at all where she'd go?" Helen asked.

Mrs Jones shook her head. "No, none at all. Actually I'd been hoping you might have some suggestions. Maybe Wendy would have talked to you about going somewhere, or mentioned a new friend."

"No, the subject has never come up. She knows plenty people, but I can't think of anyone she'd run away to at a time like this. Except me, that is, and I've not heard from her." Helen sipped her tea and the two of them sat in silence. After a minute Helen plucked up courage to ask a question which had been in her mind since lunch-time. "What did Mr Jones have to say when he heard Wendy had disappeared?"

There was a pause before the answer came. "At first he was angry, as if it was my fault that I'd allowed her to go. My fault? Huh!" Mrs Jones' voice rose as she felt a flush of anger. "I told him none of this would have happened if he hadn't dropped his bombshell on us."

Helen sat silently, not daring to comment on such a sensitive subject. Mrs Jones seemed to calm down after a moment.

"Anyway, once the news had really sunk in, I'll admit he sounded very concerned. I have to phone him if Wendy isn't home by meal-time. That's in another hour or so."

"What about the police?" asked Helen.

"We agreed we'd phone them if Wendy hasn't come home by this evening."

Silence fell again for a couple of minutes, as each became lost in her thoughts. 'How horrible all this is,' decided Helen. 'One person chooses to do what *he* wants, and suddenly everyone else's lives are devastated. Look at what it's done to Wendy, and now to her mother...'

Conversation soon restarted as they explored every possible theory on Wendy's whereabouts, managing another cup of tea each from the slowly cooling pot. Mrs Jones seemed glad of the company. Without Helen she'd have been sitting alone at that table, watching the minutes on the clock go by, hoping the door would open and her daughter walk back in.

Eventually Helen said, "I'll have to go now, I'm afraid, or my Mum will think I've gone missing too. I phoned her at lunch-time to let her know what was happening, and to make sure she was ready if Wendy turned up at our house. So she knows I was visiting here, but all the same I'd better get back now."

"Of course Helen. You head off. I'll call you as soon as Wendy comes home."

Mrs Jones was being very brave, and more than a little optimistic, Helen reckoned. She thanked her for the tea, and walked slowly back up the road, heading for her house on the outskirts. A breeze was beginning to blow, and Helen noticed the tops of the trees start to bend in the wind.

What Helen didn't see was someone crouched behind a wall just up the street. Weary and cold, carrying only a rucksack over her shoulder, the figure kept out of Helen's sight. Wendy, nowhere else to go, had had enough of walking around and was hunched there wondering whether she should simply go home.

As Helen walked past only two or three paces away, a strong urge rose in Wendy to stand up and call out to her. This was her friend - more than a friend - and she shared everything with her. No sooner had the urge surfaced

28

than Wendy buried it again. There had never been anything like this crisis before, and she had to work it out on her own. Helen moved on into the distance, unaware of how close she had come to finding the person she was so anxious about.

Nearly two hours later and Mr and Mrs Jones were combing the streets in search of Wendy. Two policemen - a detective sergeant and a constable - had been to the house already. They'd checked every room, got Mrs Jones to hunt through the photo album for an up-to-date picture of Wendy, and promised to circulate what they called a 'Missing person report' with details of what she was wearing and places she might go.

"What good will that do?" Mr Jones had asked. "It won't find my daughter."

"Well, if she's out there on the streets, one of our men might see her, so it's far from a waste of time." Detective Sergeant Turner had tried to sound reassuring. "And we'll get one or two of our men to visit key people like her closest friends and school teachers no later than tomorrow morning. That way we may track her down sooner rather than later."

"Try not to worry," the other policeman had added. "It sounds as though your daughter has decided to lodge her own protest about your family troubles. She's probably perfectly safe, and she'll be back when she's hungry enough."

"Suppose she isn't?" Mr Jones had asked.

"Let's not run ahead of the situation. If there's still no sign of her by tomorrow, we'll start looking in other ways."

To Mr and Mrs Jones it had all sounded vague and slow. They couldn't leave Wendy out all night. So now

29

they were doing their own search. Up and down the streets of the town they went, sometimes together, sometimes separately, trying to cover as much ground as possible.

Along the main street they walked, turned up a side street, looking in every doorway and shop entrance as they passed. It was around 6.45, and the temperature was dropping. "How can she be out when it's like this?" Mrs Jones said, pulling her coat more tightly around her.

"She's not thinking straight," muttered Mr Jones. "Come on, we've got to find her."

Ahead was a small cafe, the lights still on. They paused and peered through the window. Inside was a young man sweeping the floor, stacking chairs on tables. He was obviously clearing up for the night. But there was no Wendy, in fact no customers at all.

Mr and Mrs Jones moved on. There were other places to check. Less than one minute later, a small figure came round the corner, pulled open the cafe door, and stepped inside.

Bill looked up and smiled. "Hi Wendy."

"I came back. I've nowhere else to go."

"I'm glad you came. You'll be perfectly safe with me." Bill smiled, laid down his broom, and put his arm around Wendy's shoulders. "Don't you worry. I'll look after you."

CHAPTER 3

Wendy felt she was coming back to normal. Bill had brought home a couple of pizzas from the cafe, and Wendy hadn't needed asking twice to wolf one of them down. Half a packet of biscuits had followed the pizza, plus a couple of cans of Coke. 'Mum would be horrified,' Wendy thought, but managed not to feel guilty.

Now she was stretched back in a tattered arm-chair, an equally tattered black cat purring contentedly on her lap. As soon as Wendy had settled down, the cat had made itself comfortable on her.

"It's not my cat," Bill said. "He was here when I moved in, maybe left behind when the previous owners moved. I just feed it when I remember. Looks like he thinks you're his owner."

"More likely he considers he owns me," Wendy laughed. "What's his name?"

"He doesn't have a proper name. But I call him Gappy."

"Gappy? Not Puss? Or Whiskers? Why Gappy?"

"No good reason, other than that he's got one tooth missing at the front of his mouth, so it seemed appropriate."

As if on cue, the cat opened its mouth wide to yawn. "Hey, you're right! There is a tooth missing. What a

31

strange cat. Have you been in a fight Gappy?"

Gappy finished his yawn, and went back to sleep. He wasn't in a mood for conversation.

Bill's home had been only a short walk from the cafe. It was in a dead-end street, in a part of town Wendy had never seen before. The property was old and run-down. The ground level rooms, Bill had said, weren't fit to be used, and so they'd climbed a flight of stairs to the first floor where he had his living room. As they'd come into the building Wendy had noticed there were no lights on in any of the houses nearby.

She quizzed Bill. "Who owns this place? And does anyone else live around here?"

"This whole block belongs to the man who also owns the cafe. He lets me stay here for nothing because I work for him. But it won't be for long, because all these houses are due to be demolished soon. Everyone else has been rehoused, and I'll have to go in a couple of months." Bill glanced around at the peeling wallpaper, showing signs of damp in the walls. "It's not great, but I don't mind for the moment."

A nervous shiver ran down Wendy's spine. "You're the only one who lives here? There's *no-one* else nearby?"

"No-one at all. I quite like it that way."

"I don't think I would. I need to have people around."

"Well, you've got me now," Bill said warmly.

Wendy wasn't entirely reassured. She was beginning to realise just how dangerous a situation she was in. She was alone with a man she didn't really know, in a house with not another person near, and no-one knew she was there. 'It'll be alright,' she told herself. 'Bill's been so kind. He's okay.'

Weariness crept over Wendy again. It was her turn to yawn. "I think I'll need to get some sleep."

"Sure, the bed's upstairs. I'll show you."

"Goodnight Gappy," Wendy said, lifting the cat from her lap and lowering him to the floor. "I'll see you tomorrow."

Wendy followed Bill up a wooden staircase. Every tread had a creak of its own. Some of the wood had rotted, making Wendy step carefully in case her foot went right through. It was dark at the top of the stairs, and Bill had to flick the switch several times before a light came on. "Sorry, the electricity system isn't too great any more," he apologised.

Wendy nodded. There was a small top landing, and Bill led her through a door into a bedroom. Thankfully the light inside worked first time, but there wasn't much to see, only a bed, an old wardrobe, a chest of drawers, and a bedside cabinet. The carpet was threadbare in places, and the window was boarded up.

The blankets on the bed were thrown back, as if someone had just climbed out. Bill saw her looking at the tangled heap of bedcovers. "I'm afraid I'm not too good at making the bed before I go to work. I hope you don't mind."

"This is *your* bed?"

"Of course, what did you expect?"

"I thought... Well, where are you going to sleep?"

Bill laughed, a laugh which scared Wendy. "Don't worry about me. I'll be fine. You'll see."

At that, Bill left, pulling the door shut behind him. 'What have I done coming here?' Wendy asked herself. She looked around at the grubby room. There was nothing pleasant about it. She sat on the edge of the bed.

Ancient bed springs squeaked. The sheets were a dull grey colour, and Wendy wondered how long it was since they had been washed. She stood up again and walked round. The chest of drawers was covered in dust. The boards over the window were nailed in place. A stale smell filled the air. Wendy wrinkled her nose. 'I could be at home, lying on my own bed on clean sheets.' There was a clock hanging on the wall. It was 10 o'clock. There was nothing she could do to change anything that late at night. In the morning, she decided, she'd leave early and go home.

Bill had disappeared, and Wendy presumed she was meant to go to bed. She was certainly tired. Normally she did as little walking as possible, and a day of being on her feet almost constantly had worn her out.

She'd brought her rucksack upstairs with her. It had the few things in it with which she had left home. Taking another look at the bed, and still feeling nervous, she decided she wouldn't bother to put on the nightdress she had in her bag. She pulled off her heavy sweater, and decided to sleep still wearing her blouse and jeans.

She pushed off the light switch, plunging the room into almost complete darkness. The blocked-up window was letting virtually no light at all into the room. Feeling very uncomfortable, she lay down on the bed, and dragged the dirty sheets and blankets over her.

The darkness and silence were terrifying. Wendy forced her mind to shut out her fears. Instead she thought of her mother. When had she found out that Wendy hadn't gone to school? How had she reacted? Who had she told? What about her father? Had he been phoned? How did he feel about her having disappeared? Was he still with his 'girlfriend'? The thoughts tumbled round and round in her mind. Would she really go home in the morning? What would her mother say about her going away? Would she be angry or glad to have her back? Would her Dad ever come home? Did he care what happened to her?

Wendy's eyes became heavy. Tiredness rolled over her, like the tide making its way slowly but definitely up the shore. She had to sleep. Hopefully everything would seem better in the morning.

A sudden creak shattered the silence. Wendy was wide awake instantly. There it was another time! The noise was from just outside the room. Creak! The stairs! Someone was coming up the stairs..!

Terror overwhelmed Wendy. She had never known panic like this. Her heart pounded so loudly she felt the whole town must hear it. Yet she knew there was no sound other than the relentless creak of footstep following footstep up the stairs.

Wendy grabbed the pillow and held it tight. A moment later she heard the slow turning of the door handle. The hinges squeaked. Wendy saw a figure silhouetted against the light from the landing. It stood still, making no movement.

"Bill?" Wendy called. "Is that you Bill?"

There was no reply. The figure moved forward. Wendy squirmed to the far side of the bed, trying to get herself as far from this intruder as she could. A moment later and he was at the bed, and a hand stretched out towards her.

A deep, long scream formed in Wendy's throat, but she couldn't get it out. Her voice wouldn't do what she wanted it to.

"It's alright Wendy, it's only me."

"Bill? It *is* you. Oh, thank goodness for that. I was so frightened."

"You don't need to be frightened of me. I only want to take care of you." Bill laid his hand on Wendy's head, stroking her forehead gently. The panic subsided inside Wendy, and she felt a mixture of relief and exhaustion. She had been so petrified. 'For nothing...' she rebuked herself.

Wendy sank back on the bed, for a second almost oblivious to her surroundings. The soft touch of Bill's hand made her feel safe and protected, like a little girl being looked after by someone older and stronger.

She opened her eyes and smiled. "Oh Bill, I'm sorry for panicking. A lot of bad things have happened recently."

"They're all over now. Just relax, and you'll soon feel better."

Wendy lay quietly, utterly drained. Bill sat beside her, letting his fingers run through her hair. The darkness didn't seem so scary now. Maybe this was where she was meant to be. Perhaps she'd always been supposed to go into that cafe, and meet someone who would offer her a temporary home. She was secure here.

"You know, you're really pretty," Bill said. "I could be very attracted to someone like you." Wendy allowed his voice to run on. He was only saying words to make her feel better.

A moment later and she felt his fingers brush lightly over her face. His weight shifted, and she sensed him move more towards lying beside her on the bed.

Huge warning bells rang inside Wendy's head. She pulled herself away. "Bill, don't get so close. I don't like it."

"Of course you do," came his quiet voice out of the darkness. His hand stretched out again, took her by the shoulder and drew her closer to him. "All I want to do is hold you."

"No! Keep away!" Wendy said strongly. She sat up, and pushed his hand off her shoulder. "I'm grateful to you for looking after me, but what I want now is to be left alone to sleep."

Bill's voice lost its softness. "Don't *tell* me you're grateful. *Show* me. Come here." He grabbed Wendy's arm, and dragged her across the bed to him. Wendy felt Bill's other hand grip her shoulder, and she was held fast. "Now, little girl, you'll do exactly what I say," he said roughly.

"No! Get off." Wendy struggled out from under Bill's strong grasp. She made a dive for the far side of the bed. But she wasn't quick enough. His hand shot after her, got hold of her blouse, and pulled her back.

Wendy lashed out, catching Bill across the face. He yelled with pain, but held on. His fist flew in retaliation, and her head reeled as the blow landed on her cheek. His heavy arm came down across her, and his elbow pinned her to the bed. Wendy felt as if her whole chest was collapsing with the weight. Then a fist flew, and her head reeled as a blow landed on her cheek. In the darkness, she heard a dark, evil voice. "I'll show you who's boss around here..."

In that instant, Wendy knew that trusting this man had been the biggest mistake of her life. She also knew it might be the last mistake she'd ever make.

'Oh God...' she thought, words forming instantaneously and silently in her head. 'I need you, and need you now. Please,' she begged, 'please help me.'

* * * * *

Helen sat bolt upright in bed. A glance at her bedside clock told her it was 10.15. Just fifteen minutes earlier she had sunk into a deep sleep, but she was wide awake now. 'Something is wrong with Wendy, seriously wrong.' As clear as if she had heard a voice in her room, that thought had shot into her mind. With it came the certain knowledge, 'I must pray for her, and right now.'

She sat up straight in bed, and began to pray furiously. "God, please help Wendy. I don't know where she is, and I don't know what's happening, but I'm afraid she's in terrible danger. Whatever is going on, please look after her." On she went, words spilling out like water cascading over rocks. This was no time for 'learned' prayers. Helen let her heart dictate what she said. "Lord, she's been angry with you about her Mum and Dad splitting up, but you still love her. Help her now, please! Save her from whatever danger she's in. God, she needs you, she needs you this minute..."

Helen prayed as she had never prayed before. Every ounce of energy she had went into her heart's cry to God for her friend. This mattered, this really mattered. Finally, her voice trickled to a halt, and her body heaved with huge sighs. She tried to form more words, but almost none would come. The sighs turned to sobs, and tears started to roll down her cheeks. "Please, Father, please..." was all she could say. After that she sank back on her bed and cried and cried for her friend who was so lost and in such danger at that moment.

* * * * *

38

The weight of Smithers' arm lifted from Wendy's body. Her eyes had been tightly closed waiting for his other fist to strike, but the blow never came. Nervously she risked peering into the darkness. Smithers had sat up, and a second later he moved away from the bed. She didn't understand.

Then he spoke. "I'm not going to bother with you tonight. But you'll learn what happens to girls who oppose me." Then he laughed, a horrible laugh which echoed over and over in Wendy's ears as he left the room.

The door crashed behind him, followed by the ominous sound of a large lock being turned. The stairs creaked, and Wendy knew that for the moment he'd gone.

Why had he not attacked her more? Wendy was puzzled. He'd been in such a rage, and there was nothing she could have done to defend herself. Wendy had really believed she was going to die. 'Whatever made him stop, I'm glad.' Almost without thinking, more words formed in her mind, 'If you're here God, and that was you... Thank you.'

She might be safe for the moment, but Wendy knew she had to get out of that house as soon as possible. She couldn't bear the thought of hearing those creaking stairs again. What would he do next time? What had he meant when he said she'd learn what happened to girls who opposed him?

There was no point in dwelling on those questions. Wendy had to concentrate on escaping. But how was she going to do that?

She pulled herself into a seated position, and immediately gasped as a stab of pain shot across her middle. "Ouch..." she said, and folded her arms tightly in front of her. The pain was where Smithers' weight had fallen on her. She tried moving gently, and found she could although not easily. Wendy grimaced, and rubbed the area where the pain was worst, a little to one side. "That hurts..." she groaned.

She was in no position to call for a doctor, and little would be gained by feeling sorry for herself. Dragging herself off the bed, she found the light switch beside the door. How good it was to see again, even in that dingy room.

Wendy had to check if the door really was locked. She grabbed the door handle and pulled. It wouldn't move an inch. Holding her side to ease the pain, she bent down to examine the lock. It could hardly have been worse. The door had an old fashioned heavy duty lock, and the key that turned it would probably be six inches long. Wendy couldn't imagine how anyone ever needed that kind of lock on an inside door. But there it was, and it was keeping her a prisoner.

She studied the door. Maybe there were panels on it which were crumbling, and she could smash her way through. Wendy could be thoroughly unladylike if she needed to be. But that door was not going to shift for her or anyone else. It was built from ancient oak, not at all like the flimsy modern doors in her house.

'Then it'll have to be the window,' she told herself, moving across the room to see what escape possibilities were there. The boards which covered it were thick and heavy, with just tiny cracks between them. Wendy peered through. At first she could see nothing because it was night-time outside. She turned back, switched off the light in the room, and tried squinting through a crack again.

It took a minute or two for her eyes to adjust, but then she could make out one or two dim shapes. The outline of the building next door came clear. She could see its roof, and below that a row of windows. There were no lights in any of them, not surprisingly since everyone had moved out. Glancing a different way Wendy glimpsed a tiny part of the roadway, with one street light stopping the darkness consuming everything.

No-one was passing, and Wendy sighed as she realised that it was unlikely anyone would ever walk down a street which led nowhere other than to unoccupied houses.

So what mattered was whether Wendy could escape out that window. As she'd come into the building, she'd noticed that all the houses in the street looked the same. If she could work out some way down from the window of the house next door, probably she could escape the same way from her window.

The dim light from the street was just enough to provide the answer, but it wasn't a good one. Running below the windows was a tiny ledge, but it was not nearly big enough or strong enough to take her weight. She'd never be able to stand on a ledge like that. And below it was a straight drop to the ground. There was nothing else, not even a drainpipe she could climb down. If her building was the same as the one next door, she'd never escape through the window.

But she couldn't give up that easily. If she could get the wooden bars off the window, at least she'd be able to shout for help if anyone did come by. The problem was getting a grip on them to prise them off. Although there were tiny gaps between each plank, they weren't large enough for Wendy to get her fingers through. She stretched her arms wide, took hold of each end of one of the spars, and pulled. "Ow!" she shouted. For a moment she'd forgotten her side was hurt, but the strain of pulling reminded her sharply. She wouldn't try that again.

Instead Wendy grasped a plank at just one end. But it was at least two inches thick, and driven into the wooden frame with long nails. It didn't move a fraction no matter how hard she tugged. This was hopeless. She hauled on it again, wincing as pain shot through her side. "I've got to do it," she said through clenched teeth. "I've got to get free."

She clung as hard as she could to the wood, ignored the pain in her side, and pulled furiously. Nothing moved. She struggled more, and pulled harder. "Come on... *Come on...!*" she grimaced.

Suddenly Wendy's hand slipped, scraping hard against the ragged edge of the plank. The momentum of letting go unexpectedly made her lose balance, her foot slipped on the floor, and Wendy fell banging her head against the wall as she crashed downwards.

For a minute she was stunned, a dark mist swimming before her eyes. She didn't know what had happened. Reality slowly returned, and she realised she was lying in a heap on the floor. 'I hope Smithers never heard me,' she thought, terrified the noise would bring him back upstairs. Thankfully there was total silence apart from her own heavy breathing.

After a while Wendy risked trying to move. Her side hurt even more than before, but now so did her head. Her forehead ached, and touching it told her she had the beginnings of a large bruise near her eye. Her hand was sore too. She turned it over, and saw it was covered in blood. She pulled a handkerchief from her pocket, wiped the blood from her hand, and was relieved to find it had suffered nothing worse than being badly scraped. But it hurt!

Wendy hauled herself to her feet, and staggered the couple of paces back to the bed. She laid herself down as gently as she could, moving around until the pain in her side was as little as possible.

'What a mess I'm in,' Wendy told herself. 'What have I done by leaving home and coming here?'

As the minutes dragged past, Wendy relived every tortured footstep she'd taken that day as she'd walked round and round the town. When she'd reached junctions, she hadn't known whether to go left or right, and hadn't cared. Sometimes she had come back to the same crossroads later in the day, and, if she had opted for left earlier, she took right this time. What difference had it made? None at all, because she never had had anywhere specific to go. Being a runaway was utterly futile. What had it gained her? Only trouble.

The more her mind turned over all that had happened, the worse Wendy felt. Other thoughts began to surface which she'd been trying to suppress. 'Probably it's my fault that Dad left. If I'd never been born, he and Mum would have had more time for each other. They could have gone away and sorted out any problems they had. Maybe Dad wouldn't have had to work so much if he hadn't needed money for me, and for all the things I wanted.'

Part of her didn't want to believe what she was thinking, but negative ideas seemed to plant themselves and grow to full flower within seconds. She wanted to reject them, but lying there, hurt and terrified of being attacked again, she was powerless to resist and her mind surrendered to the worst. 'If I'm beaten, raped or murdered, I deserve it,' she decided. 'I've got myself into this mess by selfishness and stupidity. But maybe you meant all this, God. Maybe this is my punishment...'

With that she began to cry, every tear racking her body with pain.

CHAPTER 4

Helen woke, knowing she'd been dreaming. Normally she didn't remember anything from her dreams, but this time she felt the dream was only an inch beyond her grasp. It had something to do with Wendy, but what...?

She sat up in bed, and tried to concentrate. 'What was that dream about?' It was so frustrating. The harder she tried to gather her thoughts together, the faster they ebbed from her mind.

For five minutes she wrestled with vague memories, but all she could recollect was a building, and it was no luxury mansion. 'Just some old house which looks like it might fall down before it's knocked down,' she concluded. After another five minutes of trying to recapture indistinct images, she gave up. Whatever had been happening in the dream was gone forever. It wasn't surprising that she should have been dreaming about Wendy, but why also an old house?

Since there was probably no great significance to her dream anyway, Helen turned her attention to the new day, and tried to find the will-power to get up and get on with it. She wasn't sure what time she'd finally crawled into bed, but it had been late. Every weary muscle in her body confirmed that message to her.

Half an hour later the sound of a ringing doorbell

disturbed Helen as she was packing books into her bag ready for school. She looked at her watch. 'It's only eight o'clock. Who rings our doorbell at this time?'

She carried on getting organised, but a minute later she heard her mother call her name. "Helen, come down please. It's important."

Helen left her bag lying on the bed, glanced quickly in the mirror to see if she was even vaguely presentable, and went downstairs.

In the main room were her parents, plus three men, two of them in police uniform. "Helen," her father began, "this is Inspector Wilson, and two constables. They want to talk to you about Wendy."

Helen nodded, taken aback to be faced by a senior police officer standing in her own house.

"Good morning Helen," said the Inspector. His voice was strong and serious. "I'm sorry we have to call this early in the day, but we're anxious about your friend Wendy. I think you know she's missing...?"

"Yes," Helen said, "I was with her Mum yesterday around tea-time."

"There's still no sign of her, and her absence now is a serious matter. That's why we need to talk to you."

"I don't know how I can help," said Helen nervously, shifting her weight from one foot to the other.

"Why don't we all have a seat?" said Mrs Shaw, sensing Helen's awkwardness. "Would you like a cup of tea?"

The Inspector glared at Mrs Shaw. He wanted to get on with the interview, and didn't like to be interrupted. "I think it would be a good idea for you to go and make some tea," he said, choosing his words carefully.

Mrs Shaw sensed his displeasure, and decided not to

repeat the invitation to sit down. She beat a retreat in the direction of the kitchen.

"I have a few questions for you Helen. And," he turned in Mr Shaw's direction, "I trust I have your permission for my officers to look around?"

Helen's father was puzzled, but nodded. The two policemen immediately went up the stairs towards Helen's room.

"Why do they need to look in my room?" Helen asked.

"Just routine checking," grunted the Inspector.

"Checking for what?"

The officer seemed a little exasperated. He had come to ask questions, not answer them. "Well, young lady, it's not unknown for a girl who's vanished to be found in her best friend's bedroom, even under the bed."

"She's not here," said Helen firmly.

"That's what we're checking. But you are her best friend, I believe?"

"Yes."

"And you did have a long talk with her the evening before she disappeared?"

"Yes. I went round to her house after she phoned me."

"Tell me what you talked about."

"Lots of things, I suppose, but mostly to do with the fact that her Dad had said he was leaving home. She was very upset."

"What was she upset about?"

It sounded a strange question to Helen. "She didn't want her Dad to leave. She got on really well with him - with both her parents - and she couldn't cope with the idea of them not being together."

Footsteps sounded on the stairs behind Helen, and she glanced back to see the policemen appear at the door. They shrugged their shoulders towards the Inspector. Obviously they had found nothing. "Right lads, look around outside. Try any sheds and the like." They moved off, and the questions began again. "Did she tell you what she was going to do about her father leaving?"

Helen shook her head. "I don't think she had any idea what to do."

"Did the two of you plan anything, perhaps for her to go away for a while?"

"No, of course not. The subject of her going away never came up."

"Helen," Inspector Wilson persisted, "I must have the truth here. Did Wendy or either of you say anything about her staying away from home?"

"No. What I'm telling you is the truth. We never talked about it at all."

"Alright. We'll leave that subject for the moment." On the Inspector went with question after question about people Wendy knew, places she liked to visit, any boyfriends she had. Eventually the two other policemen returned, and the grilling came to a halt.

"We'll stop there for just now," Helen was told. "But I'll want to see you later on today. We have an incident room being set up right now down at the police station. I want you to come there later this morning and talk to one of my colleagues. We need to build up as much background information as possible about Wendy. Maybe it would be better if you didn't go to school today." For the first time Inspector Wilson smiled. "It's Friday, and not much fun sitting in a class room. Maybe an early start to the weekend isn't such bad news for you."

"Okay, I'll be along later," Helen replied, glad to find the man was almost human.

"I'm sorry to give you a hard time. But we have to get all the facts together, and we need to do it quickly."

Helen nodded. He was only trying to do his job.

"What do you think could have happened to Wendy?" Mr Shaw asked.

"Too early to guess. But I had to ask Helen so many questions because one of the first things we have to do is decide if she's simply gone off somewhere or if she's in some kind of trouble."

"The answer to that must make quite a difference to how you go about your work," Mr Shaw commented.

"Yes it does. Well, thank you both for everything."

Mrs Shaw bustled into the room, carrying a large tray filled with six cups of tea. "Tea for everyone," she announced proudly.

"Thank you Mrs Shaw, but I'm afraid we're just leaving," said the Inspector. "Perhaps another time."

"But... But I made it specially," she stammered.

The policemen were half way out the door by this time. "That was very kind of you," the Inspector said. "The good news is that you can have two cups each now. I'm sure you'll need it."

With that he was gone, before Mrs Shaw could say another word.

* * * * *

Wendy jumped as she heard the lock turn. The heavy door swung open, and there stood Smithers.

She hadn't heard him coming. For hours through the night she had lain awake, sore and scared, trying to think of some way to escape from this prison and the man who terrified her. She'd felt the minutes and hours pass more slowly than she could ever have imagined. Finally, some time after six o'clock, sleep must have engulfed her weary body. Now she was startled at Smithers' sudden entrance, and crept to the far corner of the bed on which she was sprawled.

He looked over at her and laughed roughly. "You don't look so pretty this morning. Your hair's a mess, your hand is covered in blood, and you've got a black eye. I'm not sure I want you after all."

"I certainly don't want you," Wendy spat back at him.

"Shut up. You had better show me respect and be nice to me."

Smithers moved across the room in Wendy's direction. "Get away!" Wendy shouted, cowering into a corner. "Don't come near me!"

"I'll go exactly where I like," said Smithers, sitting down on the bed. "This is my house, and this is my bed." He tossed his head, as if in disgust. "Don't say I'm not good to you. I slept on a chair downstairs last night, just so you could have a good night's sleep. Wasn't that kind?"

"If you were really kind, you'd let me go right now."

"Have I said you can't go?" Smithers put on an expression of great innocence.

Wendy straightened up, ignoring the pain she felt from her side. She began to move over the bed towards the door. A moment later Smithers grabbed her harshly, and threw her back down on the bed. "But have I said you *can* go?" he sneered at her. "I want you to get one thing straight, girl. You do what I say now. I decide if you stay and I decide if you go. I decide if you live, and I decide if..." Smithers chose not to finish the sentence, and began to laugh again.

Fear throbbed through Wendy's mind. This man was enjoying the fact that he was hurting and frightening her.

Despite her terror, a spark of defiance lit inside Wendy. "You'll never get away with this," she said forcefully. "They'll come looking for me."

"Oh yes?" Smithers said, laughing some more. "And who's going to find you here? For all they know you left town yesterday. You could be at the other end of the country by now."

Wendy lowered her eyes. The horrible truth was that he was right.

"Even if they do start looking, who's going to check this place? Everyone thinks these buildings are totally deserted."

"You still won't get away with it!" Wendy shouted.

Smithers' hand lunged forward, and took hold of her hair. She winced with pain. "Listen, you stupid girl, what I've got away with before I can get away with again. Get it into your head, you'll do what I say or you'll never do anything again."

With a final fierce tug, Smithers let go his grip, and Wendy pulled herself as far from him as the headboard on the bed would allow. Thankfully he stood up, and walked towards the door.

"I have a cafe to run. You can stay here to think things over." His lip curled, but the words came out softly. "I'll give you a little time to start being nice to me. I'm a patient man." Then his tone changed, and he snarled, "But don't let my patience run out...!"

With that he slammed the door behind him, and the heavy key was turned in the lock. Before Wendy could move the door was opened again. In the half light Smithers looked utterly evil. "I've just decided," he said. "You've got until tomorrow night at the latest. Tomorrow night... No longer." Then he pulled shut the door and locked it. His laugh echoed back up the stairs as he left the building.

Wendy sagged down on the bed, her mind and body exhausted simultaneously. Part of her was relieved that he'd gone, and part of her wanted to shriek with terror at the threats he'd made. Her body trembled as she tried to keep control of herself.

She lay back, staring at the ceiling. Suddenly a dark shadow flashed across her eyes, and a heavy weight landed on top of her. Wendy screamed! She jerked up as sharp needles pressed into her middle. They were followed by a deep "Miaowww..."

"Gappy? Is that you, Gappy?" she said, her voice shaking.

Two steely eyes stared back at her, and whiskers parted to reveal a row of less than perfect teeth. "Gappy, how did you get in here? Did you creep in while that horrible man was hurting me?" Wendy breathed out slowly, trying hard to calm down. "Of course," she said with pretend scolding, "you're not much better. You gave me such a fright jumping on me like that. And you can keep your sharp claws to yourself." She eased his weight until she was more comfortable, then sank down again, and put out a hand to stroke the cat's head. He seemed to appreciate the affection, and now that Wendy was lying still, curled up in a ball, closed his eyes, and settled for a sleep.

Once again weariness overwhelmed Wendy, and her own eyes felt heavy. "What am I going to do, Gappy?"

she said softly, running her hand through his fur. "What am I going to do?" Before she had time to panic, Wendy was asleep.

* * * * *

Inspector Wilson shifted uncomfortably in his seat. Despite all his years in the police service, he could never relax when he was meeting anxious parents for the first time. He'd handled countless cases of youngsters disappearing - he was almost an expert on such enquiries - but dealing with the real and imagined fears of a young girl's father and mother never got easier.

"I've been brought in at this early stage because I have a great deal of experience in cases like this," he was saying to Mr and Mrs Jones. "I can assure you that most times teenage girls come home very quickly." What he was not telling these parents was that he'd also been put on this enquiry so soon because in the last couple of years there had been a high number of cases in neighbouring forces where girls had never come home. Another fifteen-year-old going missing was all too sinister.

"We're grateful you're taking charge," Mr Jones said. He was slumped forward in his chair, elbows on his knees, his hands propping up his head. He had walked the streets for half the night searching for his daughter, always thinking he might find Wendy round the next corner. He'd checked every shop doorway, every bus shelter, and even every bush in the park. Finally, with nothing to show for his hours of work, complete exhaustion had taken over and he'd gone home to rest. Even then he'd hardly slept, simply lain on the couch tossing to and fro. His mind kept trying to think of any clue which would tell him where Wendy would have gone. But he had no answers. Now he stretched backwards, ran his hand through his hair and then across his unshaven face. "I'm sorry I look such a mess," he said wearily.

Inspector Wilson struggled to think up a tactful reply. An interruption from the doorbell was a welcome rescue from having to give one. Mr Jones got up to see who was calling and Mrs Jones headed for the kitchen to make coffee.

A young man stood on the doorstep, his fawn raincoat flapping round his knees. As the door opened he pushed his spectacles back from his nose, then reached into a wide pocket and pulled out a small notebook.

"Good morning Mr Jones," he said. "I'm a journalist with the local paper. I understand the police are mounting a search for your daughter who is missing. Can you confirm that?"

Mr Jones leaned against the doorpost for support. What should he tell this man? His tired mind had gone blank. "I don't think there's anything I want to say at the moment," he stumbled.

"I'm sure it would be very helpful if you did," the young reporter butted in quickly. "The right kind of publicity could mean your daughter hears how much you want her home, or help other people keep their eyes open for her."

"I suppose that's true..." Mr Jones said. "Okay, I'll answer just a few questions."

"Great! So, when did you last see Wendy?"

That was a question to be side-stepped, Mr Jones decided, for Wendy had avoided him since the scene in the kitchen a day and a half earlier. "She left for school

53

yesterday but never arrived there. And it doesn't seem as if anyone has seen her since."

"Why would she go off suddenly like that?"

It was another question Mr Jones didn't want to answer. "Maybe we'll know that when we find her," he replied, hoping the journalist didn't press the point.

"Well, where do you think she's gone, and do you think she's being kept somewhere against her will?"

"I really don't know the answer to either of these questions. She could have had an accident and be lying injured. I'll be going out later to search the woods and fields just in case."

"Do you think she's still alive?"

"What kind of question is that?" Mr Jones said angrily. "Listen, I love my daughter and of course I'm worried about her. She's never done anything like this before, and she could be in some kind of trouble now. If anyone knows anything, I'd be really grateful if they got in touch with me or with the police immediately."

The young man stood his ground. "Is it true that your daughter ran off the day after you told her your marriage was breaking up?"

The hairs tingled on the back of Mr Jones' neck, partly with tension and partly with anger. How had this journalist found that out? Why was this town so full of gossip? And what did his marriage problems have to do with finding Wendy now? But the man was waiting for an answer, and to say nothing would send its own message. He looked him straight in the eye, and forced his voice to be strong. "I don't know what stories you've been listening to, but I can tell you for sure that Mrs Jones and I are together right now searching for our daughter. Finding her and making her safe is what matters. And that's all I have to say."

"That's fine. Thanks for your help, Mr Jones. I got a picture of Wendy from the photographer who takes the school photos. We'll do our best to help you find your daughter."

Mr Jones sighed and shut his eyes momentarily, wondering if anything about his life or his family was really private any more. Then he nodded, and stepped back into the house. He closed the door, and leaned against it, relieved to have a safe refuge.

Inspector Wilson was standing further down the hallway. "I overheard most of that," he said. "You did well. You told him what you wanted to say, not what he wanted you to say. However, I'm afraid if one of them is on to the story, by the end of this morning there'll be a horde of journalists at your door or ringing you on the phone. I'll get a constable to stand at your gate and allow them through only when you're ready to talk to them. But it is worth giving them some time. Publicity might help."

They moved towards the kitchen, where Mrs Jones was pouring out the coffee for all three. "I suspect we need a bit of reviving," she said.

They perched on stools alongside the breakfast bar as hot mugs were put in front of them.

"What'll happen now?" Mrs Jones asked as they sipped their coffee.

"We have a standard procedure in cases like this," the Inspector said.

"Do you send for frogmen to search ponds and rivers?" said Mrs Jones.

The policeman smiled gently. "I think you've watched too many news bulletins or films. I hope it'll never come to that. We certainly wouldn't do anything like that at this stage, not unless we had some reason to think it necessary." Mr and Mrs Jones exchanged nervous glances. "And we don't think it's necessary just now," the Inspector added quickly. "We've other enquiries to get on with. You gave us a photograph of Wendy earlier. We have already had that copied, and my men have started going from house to house with it asking people if they've seen Wendy. Other officers are at the school, talking to all her friends there, and we'll be interviewing Helen Shaw at length again later this morning."

"Helen?" Mrs Jones interrupted. "I don't think she knows anything."

"That's for us to decide," the Inspector replied, putting on his businesslike tone of voice. "She certainly does know a great deal of useful information. It may not have to do directly with where Wendy has gone, but close friends tell each other all sorts of things. Even things parents never get to know..."

"I can believe that," murmured Mr Jones.

"There may just be something she knows about Wendy which will give us a clue. So we'll be getting as much information as we can from Helen."

"Suppose you get nowhere with all this?" asked Mrs Jones.

"One of the things I've learned is to take these matters a stage at a time. Let's get on with these enquiries for just now, and we'll worry about what comes next if we ever need to. Try and be positive. Probably before it's even lunch-time Wendy will walk back through the front door."

Mr and Mrs Jones sat with their heads bowed, saying nothing. They clearly didn't believe that last statement, and in truth neither did the Inspector.

Mr Jones looked up. "Okay, thank you for being encouraging, and we appreciate all you're doing to find our daughter." He glanced across at his wife. "We're sorry that what we did..." He hesitated, and began again. "I'm sorry that what I did made all of this happen."

He heard quiet crying beside him. He glanced at his wife, and saw tears running down her face. Inspector Wilson noticed as well, and decided it was time for him to leave. "I'll check how my officers are getting on."

"I'm really sorry," Mr Jones said when he'd gone.

Hard and angry words formed in Mrs Jones' mind, but she swallowed them down. She didn't have any energy left for that fight. "Let's just concentrate on finding Wendy," she said.

CHAPTER 5

Wendy stirred, the dreadful realisation that she was still held prisoner descending like a heavy dark blanket. She lay quietly, Gappy curled in a ball alongside her on the bed.

Her mind flooded with questions. 'Why did I ever leave home? What did I expect to achieve? Maybe I was just angry... But why, why, why did I ever agree to come here? I must have been mad. What made me think I could trust someone I'd never met before?'

More and more troubled thoughts went round and round in her mind, until Wendy couldn't stand the torture any longer. She pulled herself up and crawled off the bed.

Her side still hurt, though the pain wasn't as sharp as it had been some hours before. She felt another ache, this one in her stomach, and she realised she had eaten nothing since the pizza the night before. But hungry though she was, there was little chance of any food. She glanced at Gappy, fur tangled, tooth missing, smelling less than wonderful. Wendy managed a smile. "Don't worry. You're safe enough. I don't think I'd ever be desperate enough to eat you." Gappy raised an ear and opened one eye when she spoke, yawned, and promptly went back to sleep. He wasn't panicking.

Wendy wandered over to the chest of drawers, and

opened the top drawer. There was little in it, only several pairs of tangled socks and some underwear. The other drawers had a couple of shirts and sweaters. She pulled open the wardrobe doors. A jacket and trousers hung from hangers, and some yellowing newspapers lay in a heap on the floor. Next she checked the bedside cabinet, but it was completely empty. 'Smithers didn't bring many possessions with him,' she concluded.

She moved to the window, and peered again through the tiny crack. There was still little to be seen even though it was daylight. The houses nearby looked neglected and grim, slates already off some roofs and plaster breaking from walls. To the side was the one small area of street her angle of view would allow. It looked dirty, with litter circling as the breeze created tiny whirlwinds. The only signs of life were birds darting back and forward foraging for food. Wendy watched them for several minutes, envying their ability to launch themselves off the neighbouring roofs whenever they wanted. 'If only I could just spread wings and fly away from here,' she wished. 'I'd take off and never come near this place again.'

Wendy peered longingly through the crack between the planks of wood, her imagination enjoying the freedom which the four walls of that dingy place denied her. But her thoughts couldn't settle. Something was bothering her. She couldn't work out what it was, although she knew it had to do with what she'd seen as she looked round the room. Every item in it had been common enough, yet... It was as if a jigsaw had been put together with a piece in the wrong place. What was it about this room that didn't made sense? Finally she grasped what was troubling her: 'Why would someone take only a few clothes with him, yet bring a pile of old newspapers?' It seemed pointless, unless there was something special about those papers.

Intrigued, Wendy opened the wardrobe again, and dragged out the small heap of newspapers. She checked the dates, in case they were more recent than their appearance made them look. But none were less than six months old.

She pulled one out, and spread it open on the floor. The front page headline screamed at Wendy from large bold type: MISSING GIRL FOUND DEAD. Her eyes scanned the story. A 14-year-old girl's body had been discovered in a ditch three weeks after she'd disappeared from home. Her hand trembling with nervousness, Wendy took another newspaper from the pile. The main story was about a series of attacks late at night on young girls as they'd walked alone. The next was another gruesome report: GIRL'S BODY FOUND IN SHED. A 12-year-old had gone missing, and was never seen alive again.

Another dozen papers followed, every one of them with dramatic headlines about attacks on young girls. Some were follow-up stories. "Police admit they have no leads in the case of the murdered girl whose body was found last week..." Wendy read. None of the stories ever told of anyone being arrested for the crimes.

When she'd finished reading, Wendy sat back on the floor wishing she'd never thought to look at the newspapers. The question 'Why were they there?' hardly needed answering. She wasn't the first person this evil man had held prisoner. And he wasn't about to take pity on her and set her free. These stories told Wendy she was never likely to leave that room alive.

She felt sick. If only this was a dream, and in a few minutes she'd waken up back in her own bedroom, with all her usual things around her. She'd bounce downstairs, shout hello to her Mum and Dad, and disappear out the door to spend the day with Helen. If only...

'But I'll probably never do any of those things again,' Wendy told herself.

Dreadful thoughts poured into her mind. How had these other girls died? How much had they suffered first? What would Smithers do to her, and how would he kill her? Would her body end up in a ditch for someone to find one day, maybe weeks later? She shook her head. "I can't cope with this..." she said fiercely.

But the thoughts wouldn't disappear. If what she was going through was like a dream, then it was a nightmare. If it was like a nightmare, it was one from which she could not waken up because it was for real.

"This is me, Wendy Jones... This is happening to *me?*" she murmured with a sense of disbelief. The words came from Wendy's mouth, but seemed as if they were being spoken by someone else because dreadful experiences like this happened to others, not her. She'd heard all the warnings about strangers, and she'd watched news stories on TV of kidnaps and murders. But the people in the stories were never Wendy Jones. These things weren't part of *her* world. Who would want to imprison *her?* Who would want to harm *her?* Who would kill *her?* It had never seemed important to take the warnings seriously.

Yet all it had needed was to be in the wrong place with the wrong person just once. And now she would die because of that.

It seemed so unfair. 'Why can't I have a second

chance?' she asked herself, but no sooner had the question formed than her maturing mind told her that life simply isn't like that. Accidents happened, illness came, a mistake was made, and it would be nice to imagine that there was always an easy way out, but that was only wishful thinking. Maybe there was no way out of this trap...

Wendy closed her eyes, trying to shut out the hopelessness which came with admitting the truth. She glanced at the clock. It was eleven o'clock. 'I'd be in the English class, probably arguing with the teacher about a book,' she calculated. She worked out what class came next, and then what she'd do during the lunch-break. It was good to let at least her mind escape its prison.

Five minutes later Wendy gave up trying to keep her thoughts elsewhere. She was losing too often. Hunger, fear, the smell in the room and the shabby surroundings kept dragging her attention back.

Another thought was also fighting its way to the forefront of Wendy's attention. Locked in the bedroom, the last opportunity for Wendy to use the bathroom had been when she'd first come to the house, nearly sixteen hours previously. She'd drunk nothing that day, but the previous evening's cans of Coke were sending a strong call of nature. And the more she struggled against the need, the stronger it felt.

Perhaps she could distract herself she reckoned. She picked up her rucksack, rummaged inside, and pulled out her personal stereo. She'd made sure that came with her when she left home.

She slipped the headphones on, pushed a tape in the stereo, and lay back on the bed, letting the music wash over her. Wendy had only three tapes with her, but one followed the other, and then she began again on the first.

62

Over and over she played them until finally the small red battery light on the stereo went dim and the music became distorted.

Thankfully by then Wendy had fallen asleep.

* * * * *

It was nearly mid-day when Helen emerged from the police station. Outside she saw a familiar face. It was Fred, Wendy's friend from the school play. "Hello Helen," he called cheerily. "Any news about Wendy?"

"No, I don't think so. No-one has mentioned any new developments." Helen leaned against a wall to rest for a moment. She felt exhausted after more than an hour of being questioned.

"Do you think the police have any clues at all?" Fred asked.

"They don't seem to have. No-one can think where Wendy could have gone. I certainly don't know. She can do some crazy things, but it's not like her to get everyone worried like this."

"I agree with that. Wendy's a real live-wire, but she's not stupid."

Helen liked Fred. Some of the school's senior year never bothered with the younger pupils, as if they were 'above' talking to them. But Fred was different. He took time with everyone, and never made a fool of the person who was lost or had made a mistake.

"Why are you not at school Fred?"

"I could ask you that!"

"I'm here under police orders," Helen said with a satisfied smile. "You can't get a better excuse than that."

"Okay, but my excuse is pretty good too. Because

I'm in final year a lot of my work is on projects, and I set my own timetable. I don't have to be in school unless I have classes, and today is virtually blank. So, I thought I might be of some use to the police with the search for Wendy. I've come to offer my services."

"Fred," Helen said, grasping an idea, "would you mind helping me as I look for Wendy?"

"Sure, what do you want me to do?"

"Not a lot really. Just come with me. I'd like to search myself, but my Dad and Mum don't want me to walk around on my own until we know if there's any danger. So I need company. A bodyguard!" Helen opened her eyes wide at Fred, tried her best smile and softest voice. "You're big, strong and kind. You'll look after me, won't you?"

"Don't imagine charm will get you everywhere in life," said Fred with a mock rebuke in his voice. "But I'll help you if I can. Let me check with the police that they don't especially need me for anything, If they're not desperate, I'm your escort."

Helen nodded, and Fred disappeared inside the police station. Two minutes later and he was back. "Right, we're off, with just two conditions."

"What are they?"

"One is that you phone home first to let your parents know what we're doing. I'm not having them get anxious about you." Helen agreed. She could imagine how her mother would panic if she thought *her* daughter had disappeared as well as Wendy. "And the second condition is that we begin by getting something to eat."

"Well..." Helen hesitated.

"Don't worry, I'll pay!"

"Charm may not get me everywhere, but maybe it'll

take me a long way," Helen teased. " Where shall we go?"

"I know a little cafe up a side street. It's not great, but it's cheap. Come on..."

* * * * *

"Terrible business this about the young girl going missing" said the waiter as Fred paid him for their meal. The cafe was busy and there hadn't been time previously for conversation.

"Yes, she's a friend of ours," Fred replied. "Helen here knows her really well."

"Is that so?" came the waiter's reply. He glanced over at Helen, but she was gazing out of the window, seemingly lost in her own thoughts. Turning back to Fred, the waiter said, "Maybe you should keep your voice down, though, unless you want lots of questions from the media. More than half the people in here today are journalists or broadcasters, just turned up to cover the story. I'm sure they'd like some inside information."

Fred cast his eyes over the crowded cafe again. It was a buzz of chatter, and sure enough there were a few cameras and note books lying about. "I think we'll be happy to miss that opportunity. We'd rather use our time to do something to help find our friend."

"Quite right too."

"Hey!" a voice shouted from one of the tables. "Over here Bill!"

"Looks like I'm needed," the waiter shrugged. "Nice to see you."

"Thanks for everything," Helen called back as they left. "And, Fred," she added as they got outside, "thank you very much."

"It's my pleasure. Now, where are we going?"

"I'm not sure, but maybe we could start by walking around areas that I know Wendy likes. They're the places she'd have come to if she'd been wanting time to think."

"That makes sense to me. Lead on..."

Three hours later and they were still walking. They'd explored both banks of the river, gone through two woods, and searched every corner of the park. They'd visited three farms, the public library, and now they were back near the town centre.

"I'm sorry, Fred. This has all been a waste of time."

"You don't need to apologise. It hasn't been a waste at all. These places needed to be checked, and we've done that. It was important."

"But we're no nearer to finding Wendy," Helen said sadly.

Fred shrugged his shoulders. "In a way you're right. But the police often talk of 'eliminating people or places from their enquiries', and that's what we've been doing."

Helen smiled. "Thanks for the encouragement. I need your positive outlook at the moment."

"So, is there anywhere else today? I don't mind keeping trying if you want."

"Thanks Fred, but if I'm honest I wouldn't know where to look now. We'd just be wandering around. Besides, I'd better be getting home."

"Alright, then I'll walk you back towards your house." Helen accepted, knowing that her parents wouldn't want her to be on her own. "Let's go this way," Fred said, pointing to a small lane. "It's a short-cut."

Helen had never been along that lane before, but she was too tired to argue and followed Fred's leadership. Eyes bent to the ground and heart heavy, she walked slowly. Without planning it, she found herself praying silently. 'Lord, why couldn't we have found some clue? Wendy might be in terrible trouble, and need our help. You know where she is. Why couldn't you show us?' Helen sighed. She felt her prayer was going nowhere. There were times when God seemed deaf.

She looked up. She was among streets she'd never seen before, following Fred who seemed to know his way. Suddenly Helen stopped dead in her tracks, and stood staring.

Over to one side was a narrow side street. It appeared to lead only to a handful of old, run-down houses. Some of them - the last three or four towards the end of the street - were exactly like the house she'd seen in her dream!

Fred realised Helen had stopped, and wandered back to her. "What's up then?" he asked, seeing her gazing down the street to the side.

"I've seen one of those houses before," Helen said, pointing.

Fred frowned. "That doesn't sound a big deal."

"What I mean is, I've seen it before, but I've never been here before. It was in a dream I had last night." Helen lowered her head momentarily, thinking carefully. Then she looked along the street at the houses again, and said very deliberately, "Fred, I know it sounds silly, but could we take a look? It might be important."

* * * * *

The bird on the next house stood proudly on its chimney stack, unaware that a tired, frightened, and hungry girl was peering at it through a tiny slit in a boarded up window. The gull surveyed its world, bobbed its head once or twice, then flapped its strong wings and took off.

Wendy had watched it for the last five minutes, preferring even this tiny view of the outside world to the terror of staring at the four walls of the bedroom which locked her away. She hated that room. It not only locked her away, but now had humiliated her into squatting in a corner to relieve the irresistable call of nature. She felt embarrassed and disgusted at herself, and dreaded that she might have to do it again. Her head throbbed. She guessed it was because of the previous night's collision with the wall or something as simple as a headache brought on by hunger.

With the gull gone from the neighbouring roof, Wendy glanced down towards the part of the street within her view. Her eye caught movement. There was someone there. It was Helen! Her friend Helen was standing right outside the house in this street that no-one ever entered! A second later and Fred was beside her. She shut her eyes tight, and immediately opened them again. No, she wasn't seeing things. They were really there!

"Helen!" she screamed. "Helen! Fred! It's me, Wendy! I'm in this house. Hello! Help!"

They were paying no attention, just carrying on with their conversation.

"Helen! Helen!" she shouted as loud as she could. "I'm in here!" They were looking up at the building, sure enough, but it was in a general kind of way. Wendy could tell they had neither heard nor seen her.

"It's these bars of wood," she said. "The sound can't get through and they can't see me." With fury she battered her fists against the planks, but they were unyielding. She dug her fingernails into the wood, ignoring the pain, prising the wood backwards with all her strength. Nothing moved.

Wendy tried again, desperation taking over. She jammed her fingers into the widest gap, trying to get a proper grip. Sharp splinters of wood stabbed her fingers, but she had to get these planks off. She held on and pulled. The wood creaked. "You must move!" Wendy shrieked at it, her face contorting with effort. "You *must* move!"

There was a loud crack, and the wood snapped. Wendy fell, thrown backwards as the resistance to her pull suddenly ceased, her head crashing against the wooden leg at the corner of the bed. She lay dazed, not knowing what had happened, blood oozing from a deep cut to the back of her head.

Then her mind cleared, and she realised with growing excitement that she'd managed to rip one of the planks of wood away from the window. Wendy pulled herself up, and rushed back to the window.

The street was empty. Helen and Fred had left.

A dark and deep despair flooded over Wendy. She slumped to her knees and cried. Her head was injured. Her fingers were bleeding. And her only hope of being found had just gone.

* * * * *

"The French term for it is 'déjà vu'," Fred told Helen as they walked away from the street. "People are convinced they've seen or experienced something before, but they haven't really. I think the explanation is that one part of the brain registers an event a fraction before the next part does, so it's as if a memory of that thing already exists."

"But I dreamed about one of those houses last night."

"Or maybe you simply think you did. Your brain has to give that 'memory' some slot in time, so it's convinced you that seeing the house was part of a dream."

Helen stayed silent. She couldn't accept Fred's explanation. She *knew* she'd dreamed about the house, but she had no proof to offer and he seemed convinced by his own theory, so she didn't argue. Besides, what was the point? They'd stood and looked at old houses. Most of the windows were boarded up, and a sign nearby had said, 'Danger! Keep out. Property scheduled for demolition.' There had been no sign of Wendy, no connection with her at all. Whether she'd had a dream about one of those houses, or whether her brain was playing tricks on her, what did it matter?

CHAPTER 6

Wendy's hopes had surged when she'd seen Helen in the street. All her energy had gone into forcing the plank of wood away from the window. Now she had no strength left. She sprawled in an exhausted heap on the floor, every ounce of stamina drained from her body, excitement replaced by anger and depression.

"Why couldn't Helen and Fred have heard me?" she said. "And why couldn't they still have been there when I got that wood off the window frame?"

Wendy lay on her back and stared blankly at the ceiling. "Where are you now God? Helen tells me you care, and that you help her. So why don't you help *me?*" She sighed. "I almost thought you did something for me last night. But now...?"

She rolled over. Her hand touched one of the newspapers still lying where she'd scattered them. Without thinking, Wendy picked it up by the corner. Her eyes fell on a small box at the bottom of the front page. She read what was written there:

"For I know the plans I have for you," declares the LORD, *"plans to prosper you and not to harm you, plans to give you hope and a future."* (Jeremiah 29:11)

The words seemed to leap off the page at Wendy. She sat upright, pulled the newspaper closer, and read it again. "I wish that was true..." she said quietly. "But where is God, and why isn't he helping me escape?" The words in the newspaper couldn't be for her.

She lay down again, almost wanting to sink back into her despair. It would be easier to give up. No-one knew where she was, so no-one could rescue her. She was a prisoner of a man who was going to kill her, and there was no chance of escape. Nothing good lay ahead. She might as well die now.

'But,' part of her argued back, 'is it possible, even slightly possible, that there is a God and he knows where I am? Could he even care about me?' Phrases from that little box in the paper stuck in Wendy's mind, and she repeated them to herself, '...*the plans I have for you... plans to prosper you... not to harm you... to give you hope and a future.*' She tried to forget them, to shut them out, but round and round those words went in her head. 'They're stupid. What that 'Bible verse' says isn't true - can't be true. It doesn't make sense.' Yet, despite everything her brain told her, a tiny surge of hope ran through Wendy. Something stirred very deep inside her heart.

She stood up. Virtually the next second an idea hit her. Wendy smiled. It was crazy. It had almost no chance of success. But maybe - just maybe - it would work. She had to try.

* * * * *

"Is there any news?" Mrs Jones asked her husband anxiously, as he replaced the telephone. He'd stayed with her through the day, not going to work. "I'd never be able to concentrate," he'd said, "not when I don't know where Wendy is." There had been no mention of the 'girlfriend'. She seemed to be forgotten in the midst of the crisis.

Mr Jones shook his head, returning to his seat in the main room. "No, the Inspector says it's as if Wendy has vanished without trace."

"She can't have done that. Someone must have seen her. Someone must know where she is."

"Yes, but so far no-one has come forward with information. They've even sent men to check the local woods in case she's tried camping out. But there are no signs there of anyone having slept overnight."

"What will they do now?" Mrs Jones sounded tired. The nervous exhaustion of the last twenty four hours was taking its toll on her.

"I don't think there's anything new they can try," her husband replied. "Except publicity. Now that the press are on to the story anyway, they're using the media to publicise that she's gone missing. Apart from that, they'll simply ask more and more people if they know anything. Apparently they've already knocked on five hundred doors, and they'll keep going until they've been to every house in the town." Mr Jones slumped in a chair, feeling his own weariness. "But, if they don't turn up some real clue soon..." His voice hesitated and broke, and more words came slowly. "I'm frightened something terrible has happened to her."

* * * * *

"Okay, Gappy," Wendy said almost cheerily. "Pigeon post has been around for a long time, but you're going to be the first example ever of pussy post."

73

Gappy opened an eyelid, gave Wendy an uninterested glance, and settled back to sleep on the bed.

"I can't get out of here, but maybe you can..." Wendy had tried forcing off the other planks of wood barring the window with no success at all. They were slightly thicker than the one which had broken earlier, and the nails were firmly in the wood. So, with just one plank missing, there was only a nine inch gap. It was too small for Wendy to crawl through, but just big enough for a cat. Below the window, Wendy reckoned, had to be a ledge like the one on the neighbouring house. It would also be far too narrow for her, but not for an agile cat.

"Are you agile, though?" Wendy said doubtfully, surveying her potential rescuer curled up in a tight ball, looking all too content.

Wendy's idea was to tie a message around Gappy's neck, get him on to the ledge, and then down into the street, in hope that someone would read the message and come to her rescue. She didn't know precisely where she was, but she could give a rough description and she certainly knew the cafe to which the police should go to find the man who had captured her.

The biggest problem, Wendy realised, was how Gappy would get down off the ledge. It was too high to jump. Not even a light footed cat would survive the drop. Wendy had to hope that the ledge ran round the house, and perhaps Gappy would be able to escape by getting on to the roof of another building, or clambering down on to an outhouse. There wasn't a high probability of success, but it was the only chance she had.

"Okay, let's write out a message," she announced to Gappy who remained blissfully unaware of his hazardous future.

Wendy rummaged in her rucksack for a pen. She knew she didn't have any paper, but there were plenty sheets of newspaper around. She could rip a page apart, and write on it. She felt around among the few clothes she had brought, but her hand couldn't find the pen. With a ball of anxiety growing in her stomach, she hurriedly tipped everything out on to the floor. She pulled aside her couple of sweaters, change of underwear and extra pair of jeans. She checked inside the folds of the clothes, but there was no pen! She had forgotten to bring it.

'Maybe there's one somewhere else in this room,' she thought hopefully.

She pulled open the drawers, searched every corner of the wardrobe, and looked inside the bedside cabinet. There was nothing with which she could write. She scoured every inch of the rucksack again, and looked a second time through every piece of clothing. But still there was nothing. Wendy sat back on her ankles, and groaned. Her idea couldn't die before it was even born.

Suddenly a smile crossed her face. "I'll tape my message," she announced to herself. Wendy's personal stereo didn't merely play tapes, it had a record button and a small, built-in microphone.

She picked up the stereo from where it had slipped off the bed on to the floor, slid in a cassette, and pushed the record button. It wouldn't move. She tried again, using more force. It didn't budge.

"What's wrong with it?" she muttered. Then it dawned on her. The cassette was pre-recorded, and that meant the small tab on the back on the cassette had been broken off to make sure no-one accidentally taped over it. Without the tab in place, the record mechanism on her stereo wouldn't work.

Wendy pulled out the cassette again, and studied the back of it. Where the tab would have been, there was now a small hole. 'Why don't I just fill the hole?' she asked herself.

She tore a small strip from one of the newspapers, rolled it into a ball, and jammed it into the gap. The cassette went back into the machine, Wendy pressed the button, and down it went. "Great!" she said enthusiastically, switching off again until she was ready.

Wendy sat down on the bed, and thought carefully what she wanted to say. She needed to tell people what had happened to her, and where she was.

Two minutes later she was ready. She raised the tape player nearer to her mouth, pressed the record button, saw the little red light come on, and began: "This is Wendy Jones. I'm being kept a prisoner by a madman who's going to kill me by tomorrow night. His name is Bill, and he works in the cafe up the side street beside the town centre. Bill Smithers is his full name and he's keeping me a prisoner in his house which is only a couple of streets away from the cafe. All the houses here are boarded up, because they're going to be pulled down soon. Please help! Tell the police where I am!"

She paused, thinking what to say next. As she lowered the cassette recorder, she noticed the red light had gone out. She looked closer. The tape wasn't turning.

"That's funny," Wendy said. "I know it started to record." She shook her stereo, switched it off and then on again, but there were no signs of life. She tried another time. Still nothing.

Then it dawned on her. The batteries were dead. She'd used the stereo earlier, and remembered she'd fallen asleep listening to it. 'I must have used up all its power. Maybe there was a tiny bit left, enough to get it going, but that's all. So how much did it record?'

That was the crucial question, but without battery power she had no way to check. There was no choice but to hope enough information had gone on the tape to bring help.

She took the tape from the stereo, pulled a lace from her shoe, and then placed Gappy on her lap. He stretched his legs, unsure why his sleep had been disturbed.

Wendy threaded the end of the lace through one of the sprocket holes of the cassette, and then tied the lace around Gappy's neck, leaving the cassette dangling below him. The cat twisted his head, unused to having a tape hung from him. He lifted a paw, and pushed it against the cassette, as if to dislodge it.

"Oh no, you mustn't do that," Wendy rebuked him, and retied the lace tighter so that there was no space left for Gappy to get his paw in and pull the tape off.

A few seconds later and she was ready. She moved over to the window. "God, if you're there," she breathed near silently, "please make this message reach someone who'll understand and help."

The gap in the planks wasn't enough for her to be able to reach through and open the window. Wendy wasn't put off. She took her shoe, slid her arm through, and used the heel of the shoe to smash the pane of glass. There was a loud crash, and glass fell down to the street. Wendy knocked out other sharp edges, making the hole as large as she could.

She picked up Gappy, and hugged him close. "Do your best for me, friend," she murmured over him.

Then she lifted him up to the gap in the wood. Gappy

didn't like the idea of being squeezed through the small space, and wriggled violently. "Come on, it'll be okay," Wendy coaxed. She helped his head through, and somehow Gappy's body followed.

Wendy's arm was just long enough to reach beyond the broken pane, and she laid Gappy down on the window frame. He looked round at her, as if to say, "What am I doing out here?"

"Go on," Wendy urged.

Gappy seemed to understand. A second later, he stepped delicately off the window frame, and Wendy knew he must have gone on to the ledge. She craned her head to try and squint down, but the ledge was below the line of the window and she couldn't see him.

"I hope you're alright," Wendy sighed. There was nothing more she could do.

She was about to turn away from the window, when she heard a loud, screeched "Miaowww...", a scrabbling as if paws were trying to get a grip on stone, and a second later a crashing sound. She knew what it meant. Gappy had fallen. Her message - and messenger - had died.

* * * * *

"Come on, dear, you've hardly touched your meal." Helen's mother looked anxiously across the table at her daughter, who sat picking idly at her food.

"I'm not really hungry, thanks."

"I know, but you've got to eat."

Helen smiled half-heartedly at her mother, grateful for her concern. But her appetite simply wasn't there. Deep in her bones, she knew her best friend was in trouble. She didn't know what kind of trouble. She could be lost, hurt, or in danger from someone. Whatever it was, it was serious, and Helen couldn't just carry on with life as if nothing had happened.

Her father joined the conversation. "Have you had any more ideas where Wendy might have gone?"

"No," Helen replied, shaking her head. "The more I've thought about it, the more I know she wouldn't stay away from home. She might disappear for a few hours if she was upset. But that's it. She wouldn't want to worry her parents, and, besides, she likes her home comforts too much."

"I wonder what she's getting to eat?" Mrs Shaw said, thinking of practicalities.

"I hope she's got somewhere proper to sleep," her husband added. "I'd hate to think she was trying to camp out in the open. Often people don't realise how dangerous the cold can be."

"But she wouldn't stay out. That's just not Wendy. Someone must be keeping her prisoner," said Helen.

"Surely Wendy wouldn't go off with a stranger, though," said Mrs Shaw. "She must have been taught not to do that."

Helen shrugged. "I'm sure she's been told plenty times, like you've told me. But you know Wendy. She's always full of confidence, and she'd never believe anything bad could happen to her."

"No-one ever thinks it can happen to them, until it does," Mr Shaw said seriously.

The conversation stopped. Helen pushed the food around her plate for another minute or two, then laid down her knife and fork beside the half-eaten meal. "I'm sorry, Mum, I can't eat any more."

"That's okay. Maybe you'll want something later."

"Helen, is there anything we could do to help find Wendy?" asked Mr Shaw. He was a thoughtful man, and knew that what his daughter needed more than anything was to do something for her friend.

"I don't know, Dad. I walked around with Fred for ages today, looking for some clue to where she'd gone. I'm not sure what I expected to find, but there was nothing."

Her father nodded. "It was important to try."

"There was just one moment..." Helen added, unsure if she should try and explain about the strange way she'd recognised a building. She decided to take the risk. "At one point I felt I was standing before some houses which seemed special."

"What do you mean 'special'?" her mother asked.

"I don't know, Mum. That's the frustrating thing. I had a vivid dream last night, which I think was connected with Wendy. But the only thing I can remember from the dream was a house. When I was with Fred we came across some houses just like the one I saw in my dream."

"And you think that's where Wendy could be?" asked Mr Shaw.

"Well, no, she can't be. They're all boarded up, probably ready to be knocked down. There's no-one living there. But it seemed strange that I saw those houses in my dream when I'd never been in that part of town before."

"What did Fred think?"

"He said I was experiencing 'déjà vu', that I only imagined I'd seen them in the dream, and really it was my brain playing tricks on me."

"Do you believe that?" pressed her father.

Helen wrinkled up her nose. "He could be right, I

suppose." She smiled. "But I'm not convinced."

"No, that doesn't surprise me. When you believe something it takes a lot to persuade you otherwise. Listen, Helen, would it help if the two of us went for a walk this evening so you can show me the house that was in your dream?"

"Could we do that Dad?"

"Well, I'm fit enough for it, but, of course, if a youngster like you hasn't got the stamina..."

"Let's go!" said Helen, jumping up from the table and making for the door.

Mr Shaw glanced over at his wife. "Don't worry," she said. "I'll clear up from our meal. Off you go the pair of you."

"Just give me a chance to get my coat," Mr Shaw shouted after Helen.

"Okay, but come on. This is important!"

* * * * *

Smithers looked at his watch. It was 6.30, just half-an-hour before he could close the cafe. There were only a handful of customers still sitting at tables, and he knew it was unlikely any more would come in now.

'I should get closed on time,' he reckoned. 'There isn't much clearing up to do either, so I'll get away sharply.'

One or two called to him for another coffee or a final burger. He fetched their orders quickly, chatting cheerily to his customers as he served them. "Thanks Bill," one of them said. "You're a good guy. I wish there were more like you around."

Smithers liked that. He needed people to think highly

of him. In a few minutes he'd be able to go home and make sure that stubborn girl Wendy appreciated him as well. Whatever it took, she'd do what he wanted.

He smiled. Nothing would bring him greater pleasure than that.

CHAPTER 7

The distant sound of the house door being unlocked sent a wave of fear crashing over Wendy. 'I mustn't panic,' she told herself desperately. She had done little in the last two hours other than think how she would cope with Smithers getting home. Wendy knew she must not make him angry, because then he might get violent and anything could happen. Instead, she'd be calm, pleasant and persuasive. 'Maybe,' she thought, 'I can make him see that he should just let me go. Surely he would realise that that would be better for him than adding to his crimes.'

Wendy heard the outside door slam, and the sound of footsteps going into the room below. She crouched in a corner, waiting for the creak of the stairs, but it didn't come. Instead there was the noise of pots and pans being moved around. Smithers was making himself a meal.

The pain of hunger gnawed at Wendy's stomach. She had had nothing to eat or drink for nearly twenty four hours, and now hunger combined with fear made Wendy feel sick. When she allowed herself to think about it, her head still hurt and so did her side where she'd been pinned down the previous night.

A cold draught blew through the gap in the window, causing Wendy to shiver and fold her arms tightly across herself to try and keep warm. She stared at the floor.

What was her Mum thinking? Where was her Dad? Was he interested that she'd gone from home? Did he even know? Maybe her Mum hadn't bothered to tell him. She felt guilty about Helen. She'd shared virtually every secret she'd ever had with her best friend, but this time she'd crouched behind a wall and allowed Helen to walk past. What kind of friend was she to Helen?

Self-condemnation mixed with self-pity enveloped Wendy like a dark and impenetrable mist. 'Maybe they've all given up on me. I may not come out of this alive, and if I do, who'll care? Who's bothered about me, even now?'

* * * * *

Helen hurried towards the town centre, her father doing his best to keep up with his anxious daughter. "Not so fast, Helen," he gasped. "I know you're worried, but you'll wear me into the ground going at this speed."

"I'm sorry," Helen said, slowing down for about ten paces before speeding up again. Mr Shaw smiled as he quickened his stride to stay with her. He remembered only a few years back, when it was Helen's little feet which had had to go at double speed to keep up with him. Now the situation had almost reversed.

They wound their way through a maze of streets, Helen making a beeline for the row of old houses she'd seen earlier. There had to be some significance to them. If anyone had asked her to explain how she knew that, she couldn't have answered. But deep inside, there was something about these houses which was connected with Wendy's disappearance.

At last they reached the right area, and Helen pointed

down the small cul-de-sac towards the boarded up houses. "That's them, Dad. That row of old homes."

Her father stood looking carefully at them. "I remember something in the newspaper about these houses," he said, trying to recall the details. "I think the local authority ruled they were no longer fit for people to live in, and put a demolition order on them. The only thing left to be decided is what's to be built on this site instead of them."

"So everyone has been moved out now?"

"Yes, no-one should be living here any more."

They walked slowly down the old street, looking closely at each of the houses. Most were in poor condition. Broken slates lay on the ground where they had fallen from roofs. In places the guttering hung at crazy angles because supports had rusted away. Most of the glass was smashed in the windows, though they were nearly all boarded up anyway.

They turned at the end of the street, and began to walk back. "Does any particular house stand out for you?" asked Mr Shaw.

Helen shrugged with frustration. "I'm not sure." She pointed one out. "This house is in the right place in the street from what I remember, but in the dream I was looking at a house of a specific style, and all these houses are of that style. I keep trying to pick out special details. But, I couldn't say any one of these houses is different from the rest."

They stepped carefully over some broken rubble and slates, ducked under the branches of a tree, and moved round the side of one of the houses. Clambering over a low wall, they gazed up at the back of the building.

There were no signs of life. "I don't think we're going

to find anything," said Mr Shaw. "Maybe Fred's right with his déjà vu theory."

"Maybe," Helen grunted.

They found their way again to the street, and as they moved away Helen glanced back over her shoulder toward the house. Suddenly she stiffened. Her eye had caught a movement.

"Dad! Dad! I saw something - someone - at a window. There's someone in that house."

"Are you sure Helen? Where about?"

She pointed out a window. "It was up there. I'm sure there was someone. Do you think...?"

"Helen, if there was someone there, it could be anyone. Maybe tramps have broken in, just wanting to keep warm and dry." But Mr Shaw knew that answer would never satisfy his daughter. "Okay, I'll try banging on the door and we'll see if anyone answers."

Mr Shaw led the way to the main door of the house. A large knocker hung from the door. He brought it crashing down several times, the bang echoing inside the house. "Sounds deserted in there," he said.

There was silence, no sound of footsteps coming towards the door. "Try again," Helen urged.

The door knocker clattered down another three times, as hard as Mr Shaw dared. He thought it might splinter the wood if he banged it any harder. The sound echoed inside, suggesting there were no carpets or other furnishings to deaden the reverberation.

"I think we'll have to go..." Mr Shaw was saying, when both of them heard a faint noise of feet in the distance. The footsteps got louder. They were coming down wooden stairs. Helen's heart thumped ever louder in unison with the footsteps.

With a heavy creak, the door opened, and a face peered out at them.

* * * * *

"So, what have we achieved today?" Inspector Wilson had gathered his main team of police officers for an end of day briefing. They were strangely quiet. When an enquiry was making progress, there was always a buzz of excitement when the team came together. Everyone had snippets of news to pass on. But the twenty who stood passively in the incident room in the local police station were not in that kind of mood. They knew they were little further forward than when they started that morning. "Let's assemble the things we know," said the Inspector.

He took some chalk, and moved to a large blackboard mounted on the wall. "We have only a few key facts so far. First, we know there was a family crisis." In large letters he wrote FAMILY CRISIS on his board. "Mr Jones had told his wife and daughter he was leaving them, and we have evidence from Helen Shaw that Wendy took that news very badly. Now, what else do we have?"

Twenty faces looked at him blankly. They had scoured the streets, interviewed hundreds of people at their homes, begun to search woodland, and put out appeals via the media, but had drawn a complete blank on clues to Wendy Jones' whereabouts. "No joy, sir. No-one seems to have seen the girl," came one weary voice.

"Alright, I know it's negative, but that's still a significant fact." NO SIGHTINGS was written on the board. "What else?" the Inspector asked.

"I went to the school," said Sergeant Turner. "I talked with the headmaster, teachers, and some pupils.

Wendy was well liked and the standard of her work was above average. She was playing a leading part in the school play, and everyone said she was looking forward to that. As far as school is concerned, there were more reasons for her to stay than to run away."

Another police officer joined in. "Helen Shaw seems to have been a particularly close friend to Wendy. It's not as if she had no-one to talk to."

"Fine, we're making progress," Inspector Wilson said. He wrote GOOD AT SCHOOL and WELL LIKED on the board, and after a moment added CLOSE FRIEND. He stood back and studied what he'd written. "Are there any more facts we should put there?" he asked.

No-one answered. "I've one more of my own," said the Inspector. "Isn't it true that quite a number have said Wendy was a confident, talkative, outgoing kind of girl?"

Several people nodded. One officer chipped in, "Someone said you only need ears when you're around Wendy Jones since *you* won't be doing any of the talking." The group smiled.

"Okay," Inspector Wilson said quickly, anxious to keep the meeting on track. "Let's write OUTGOING PERSONALITY on our list," and he added the words to the board.

He moved away from the blackboard again, and examined the final result. "So," he said, "we may not have much, but we do have some clues among these facts. Correct me if I go wrong... We know Wendy was upset, and probably walked out yesterday morning in protest. There don't seem to have been any other big problems in her life, so she was reacting to the break-up of the family."

Every head nodded in agreement. None of them were likely to argue with Inspector Wilson anyway.

"The next important fact is that no-one either knew where she was going nor has seen her since. There are good reasons why she would have come home soon. And if Wendy had been planning to stay away for a long time, wouldn't she have told her closest friend? But Helen Shaw didn't know. And if she'd gone to anyone's home in the town, or been given a lift to somewhere else, wouldn't we have heard by now? After all our interviewing, the publicity that's gone out now that the media are on to the story, and the gossip that goes round a town like this like lightning, it would be hard for anyone not to be aware that we're searching for this girl."

"Perhaps someone hasn't been watching TV today or hasn't read the evening paper, so doesn't realise Wendy is missing," one policeman dared to say.

"Perhaps..." the Inspector conceded. "But that's not the most likely explanation. What's more likely is that whoever has seen Wendy Jones doesn't want to tell us."

"Or..." the policeman ventured again.

"Or?" Inspector Wilson growled.

"Or she's dead," came the stark words.

The Inspector frowned. "Yes," he said wearily. "She could be dead - had an accident or killed herself somewhere remote and we haven't found her body yet." His voice strengthened. "But until we do find a body, we'll assume Wendy Jones is alive, perhaps held against her will, and we'll keep searching until we find her."

* * * * *

"I'm so sorry to bother you," Mr Shaw said to the young man whose face peered round the door. Helen recognised him vaguely though wasn't sure how. Meanwhile her father searched desperately for words. "It's just that... Em, well, we didn't think anyone lived here any more." Even as he spoke, Mr Shaw realised what a poor explanation that was for banging on someone's door.

"Well, as you can see, I live here," said the man, his voice sounding so polite his callers could never have realised how unwelcome they were. "I will be here for only a few more weeks, but I can assure you I have every right to stay in this building. I can give you my landlord's address if you want to check."

"No, no, that won't be necessary," Mr Shaw said apologetically. "I have no reason to doubt you." He hesitated, before continuing. "Actually, we're looking for my daughter's friend, a girl called Wendy. You wouldn't have any idea where she could be would you?"

"I'm sorry, none at all," the young man said, with a real look of concern on his face. "I'd heard a young girl had gone missing. It sounds serious." He looked down at Helen. "You must be worried about your friend." Helen nodded glumly, but said nothing.

"Well, thank you for your help," Mr Shaw said. "We'd better be getting along. Again, I'm very sorry for disturbing you."

"That's no problem," the young man replied. "Good night."

Helen and her father walked away, feeling embarrassed and awkward about the conversation. Bill Smithers closed the door, smiled to himself, and climbed back up the stairs. He went past his main room, up the second flight of stairs, and into his bedroom. Wendy lay on the bed, her hands and feet tied tightly with rope, and a gag over her mouth. Along with a beating, it was the price she'd paid for pulling the spar from the window. Smithers was making sure she'd never again try to attract attention.

Now he looked down at the helpless and terrified girl, and laughed. "It seems I sorted you out just in time. That was your friend and her father at my door. But it was easy getting rid of them. No-one will come here again to look for you."

CHAPTER 8

"I felt so embarrassed," said Mr Shaw as they walked away from the house. "I didn't know what to say to that young man when he came to the door. I had no right to ask him why he was living there, or any other question for that matter."

Helen was silent, trying hard to recall where she'd seen the man's face before. She could picture him doing something, but what was it and where was it? The image wouldn't come to the front of her mind. She wished she paid more attention to people around her. 'It doesn't matter,' she reassured herself. Her town wasn't all that big, and it was a common enough experience to half-recognise a face without knowing who the person was.

"We need to get home now, get a warm drink, and then you should be off to bed," Mr Shaw said. "You've done a lot of walking today. Are you feeling tired?"

"A bit," Helen said, not wanting to admit how exhausted she really felt. She knew that a large part of her tiredness was disappointment that there had been no news at all of Wendy.

Out on to the main street they walked, and back up the hill away from the town. Helen kept her head down, staring at the ground, her mind absorbed in its own thoughts. Her inattention meant she never saw a small furry obstacle in her path until it was too late. There was a loud squeal "Miaowww...!" as Helen's foot barged into the black cat.

"Oh, sorry!" Helen said to the cat as she struggled to regain her balance. The cat scampered a few metres away, and as it did so Helen and her father heard a strange rattling sound, as if something was being dragged along the ground.

"The poor cat has got something caught round his neck," said Mr Shaw. "He could choke. Try to catch him, Helen, and we'll untie him."

Helen bent forward. "Come here, little pussy cat." She rustled her fingers gently, and spoke softly. "Come on. We'll help you."

"Miaow..." came the reply, and the cat moved another few metres away, pulling something along after it. Even in the evening gloom, Helen could see that the cat was also limping.

"It looks like he's wrapped himself in an old cassette," Helen said. "And I think he's hurt himself." She spoke to the cat again. "Come on. Come and get some help."

Gappy was no fool of a cat. He'd spent most of his days scrounging food and affection from anyone he could. So he wasn't going to play hard to get any longer, and turned back in Helen's direction. "Miaow, miaow..." he murmured.

Helen folded the cat in her arms, held him close and stroked his ears. A gentle purring told her the cat was sufficiently grateful.

"How did you manage to get yourself all tangled up with a cassette?" Helen asked her new friend. But it took only a second for Helen to see her first assumption was wrong. The cat's head was not wrapped in cassette tape

- the cassette was firmly tied to the cat with the lace from a shoe.

"Who could have done that?" said Mr Shaw angrily. "They might have hurt the cat. And why would someone tie a cassette round his neck?"

"I don't think the cord has done the cat any harm, Dad," said Helen, carrying out an inspection. "But his fur is torn, there's a twig stuck in his back, and I think he's damaged at least one of his paws. Well," she added soothingly, "we'll look after you."

Helen eased the twig out of the cat's fur, grateful that only a tiny wound was left. Then her neat fingers unpicked the knot, and the lace was released. Gappy shook his head, glad to be free of the tight cord and the weight of the cassette tape.

"Okay, Helen, before you ask, yes you can take the cat home at least for tonight to give him some milk and food. But we must go now. There's a refuse bin over there. Throw the tape and the lace in it and let's get up the road."

"Hold on, I might like the cassette. What is it?" Helen was teasing her father. She squinted her eyes in the dark to make out the name on the label. "It's 'Abba Gold'," she said. "Don't panic. That's not my kind of music, Dad. But Wendy never stops listening to it. It's one of her favourites..."

Helen's words trailed off, and she stared down at the cassette. Her father had also halted in his tracks. The same wild idea had crossed both their minds simultaneously. Without saying another word, they turned and headed straight for the police station.

* * * * *

94

The rope cut deep into Wendy's wrists and ankles. She'd tried to wriggle free, but all she'd managed to do was rub her skin raw. Although she couldn't see it, she knew her face had been bleeding where Smithers had hit her, and she felt sore from bruises on several parts of her body where his blows had also landed. The rag tied over her mouth was making it hard to breathe.

Trying to get help had nearly cost Wendy her life. Smithers had exploded with anger when he found one of the spars missing from the window, and the pane of glass broken. "You little tramp!" he'd shouted. "Did you think you might escape? Did you think someone would come along and find you here?" On and on he'd ranted about how she was in his power, and how ungrateful she was to him for taking her in when she'd nowhere else to go. "You're mine! Only mine!" he'd yelled. "And I'll show you that I can do anything I please with you." A second later and Wendy was being treated like a boxer's punch bag, as heavy blows rained down on her. Cowering in a corner, she'd tried to put up her arms to protect herself, but the punches had still hit her body. She'd kept her head down, until he'd paused. Then she'd glanced up, a bad mistake, as she saw Smithers' massive fist coming straight for her. Then she remembered no more.

It couldn't have been long before she'd regained consciousness, but by then she was lying on the bed, tied and gagged. Smithers had a heavy hammer in his hand, and was banging long nails into a new piece of wood to board up the window again. When he saw her awake, he'd waved the hammer at her and made it clear that he'd use it on her head if she tried to pull any more boards clear of the window. Meanwhile she wasn't going to get the chance, for he'd leave her tied up.

Now Wendy was alone and lay crying quietly to herself. In the distance she'd heard someone banging at the door of the house, and Smithers sending him away. She felt numb when she found out it had been Helen and her father. It was just one more agony to add to all the others. Why couldn't they have come a couple of hours earlier, when she'd still been on her own? She could have done something then to attract their attention, and she'd have been out of her prison by now.

Instead they'd been sent away, reassured that she wasn't there. Now they'd never look in that street again. No-one was going to find her before she died.

* * * * *

Inspector Wilson reached the safety of his car. At last he'd escaped from journalists, ringing phones, and the countless reports police officers had laid on his desk. There were summaries of interviews, background notes on Wendy Jones, and details of every case of abduction for the past five years. But now, finally, he could go home for a little while. It had been a long hard day, and tomorrow wasn't shaping up to be any easier.

The engine burst into life, and he pulled out of his parking place, heading for the exit from the car park. Suddenly two shapes darted in front of him. His foot rammed on the brake, and the car jerked to a halt. The Inspector felt his heart pounding at the near miss. Almost instinctively he rolled down his window, and shouted to the man and girl, "You stupid pair! Why don't you look where you're going? I could have run over you!"

"Inspector Wilson!" came Helen's bright voice. "Just the man we came to see."

The Inspector's heart sank. He'd already phoned his wife to tell her to prepare his evening meal. He could almost smell the succulent steak cooking under the grill, and just about taste every mouthful already. Now he felt the bubble of anticipation burst. "Hello Helen. Hello Mr Shaw."

"We think we've found something important," Helen said quickly.

"Important enough to kill yourselves in front of my car?" the Inspector asked dryly.

"I'm sorry about that," interjected Mr Shaw. "We were in a hurry to find you."

"Well, now you have," replied the police officer in a resigned tone. "But we can't hold a conversation through a car window. I'll park my car again, and we can all go inside."

A few minutes later, and they were seated inside the main incident room where a smaller evening staff were on duty to handle any overnight developments.

"What have you come up with then?" he asked. "Apart from a rather bedraggled looking cat..." he added, looking curiously at Gappy's toothless grin as he lay in Helen's arms.

"It's not the cat," said Mr Shaw, "but what the cat had tied to it which matters." He handed over the cassette. "That tape was hung round the cat's neck."

The Inspector gave it a glance. "So?"

"So it's a tape by Abba..." Helen said, as if the importance of that was obvious.

"I have heard of them," the Inspector said sarcastically. "But I fail to see what a Swedish pop group has to do with my enquiries."

"Well, Abba is Wendy's favourite group. Maybe she

sent the tape out to us to show she's still alive!" But, as she listened to her own words, Helen realised how feeble such a theory sounded. "She could have meant that, couldn't she?"

"Anything's possible," replied Inspector Wilson, holding the tape carefully. "The shiny surface of the side of the cassette might have been good for getting fingerprints, but I suspect yours are all over it by now." Helen's face fell. That had never occurred to her.

"But doesn't the fact that a tape which Wendy likes was tied to a cat's neck mean something by itself?" asked Mr Shaw.

"Does it?" asked the Inspector bluntly, feeling the weariness of the day. "We'll check with Mr and Mrs Jones to see if this tape is missing from Wendy's room. But, Helen, how many of your friends have this tape?"

Helen thought. "I guess at least half in my class own it," she admitted eventually.

"That's what I thought. So even if Wendy did go off with her own copy, this tape could belong to anyone." The Inspector looked across the desk at two disappointed faces. "I'm sorry," he said, "but we must deal with facts. We can't turn something into a clue when it isn't one."

They all sat quietly for a moment, Helen and her father allowing the truth to sink in that finding a tape tied to a cat wasn't much of a clue for anything. Yet, Helen reckoned, it was strange. People don't tie tapes to cats! There had to be more to this than they knew yet.

She broke the silence. "Could we try listening to the tape?"

"Helen, we can't keep Inspector Wilson back any longer," her father said.

"No, it's alright," the Inspector replied with unusual

kindness. "If it helps satisfy Helen we can listen for a moment. We have a tape recorder here which we use for recording interviews." He opened a small cupboard, and pulled the tape player out on to his desk. He slipped the tape into the machine, pressed the button, and four Swedish voices boomed out the lyrics of *Dancing Queen*. Other policemen and women turned their heads, curious to know what had possessed their boss to play pop music.

"See," he said, turning the tape off. "It's just an ordinary cassette."

"It didn't start from the beginning. Try rewinding it and playing it again," said Helen, risking rudeness by giving orders to the police officer.

Thankfully Inspector Wilson only smiled at Helen's assertiveness. He pushed the rewind button, waited the few seconds while the tape ran back, and then pressed play again.

There was a quiet hiss as the leader tape ran through. Then a voice very familiar to Helen broke the silence.

* * * * *

The sound of the phone made Mr Jones jump. He'd been dozing in his armchair, exhausted after virtually no sleep the previous night and a day spent dealing with the press and searching all over town for his daughter. A heavy meal followed by a comfortable chair had been enough to send him to sleep. In a second he was awake, though, and had the phone in his hand.

"Hello?" he said, hoping there would be news of Wendy, and not merely another reporter wanting a statement from him.

"Inspector Wilson here, Mr Jones. We'd like you and

your wife to come down to the police station please."

"Have you found Wendy, Inspector?"

"No, but we are further on with our enquiries. We'd be grateful if you could come now."

"We'll be there in five minutes."

* * * * *

"It's a shame there isn't more on the tape. I have a feeling my officers could be collecting your daughter right now if she'd been able to record the whole of her message. But she must have been interrupted or something went wrong with her tape recorder, so we have only the beginning of what she said." Inspector Wilson had already explained Helen's find to Mr and Mrs Jones who didn't know whether to respond with excitement or disappointment.

"Does the tape tell us where she is?" Mr Jones asked anxiously.

"Not really," replied the Inspector. "I'll let you hear what we have. It's short, but you may not find this easy," he warned.

Mrs Jones closed her eyes. She wanted to concentrate on listening, but she was frightened what she was going to hear.

The tape hissed, and then crackled into life. The voice sounded weak, but it was unmistakable. *This is Wendy Jones. I'm being kept a prisoner by a madman who's going to kill me by tomorrow night. His name is Bill, and he...* The voice ended, and Abba's music played. The Inspector pushed the stop button.

A quiet sobbing came from behind Mrs Jones' hands which covered her face. Instinctively her husband put a protective arm around her, and she didn't object. "Is that all there is?" he asked.

"I'm afraid so. I wish there was more. However, wishing won't get us far." Inspector Wilson leaned back in his chair. "I need answers to some questions."

"Of course. Ask anything at all."

"First, that is Wendy isn't it?"

"Yes," came the anguished voice of Mrs Jones. "That's her. That's *her!*" she said, struggling to keep control.

"Right," the Inspector interjected quickly, wanting to hold the conversation together. "Who's Bill?"

Mr Jones hunched his shoulders. "The name means nothing to me, but, I'll admit I don't know many of Wendy's friends. Perhaps my wife knows..." A shaken head indicated that the name was equally unfamiliar to Mrs Jones.

"Think carefully," Inspector Wilson urged. "Did Wendy mention anyone by that name, perhaps just in the last week?"

"No, I'm sorry, it doesn't ring any bells at all," Mrs Jones said, recovering most of her composure. "Maybe others will recognise the name, though."

"We'll be asking them," reassured the Inspector. "And we'll be doing it tonight. All my officers are being called back on duty, and they'll visit again every significant contact. There's a reasonable chance someone will know who he is."

"And if not?" asked Mr Jones.

"If not, we'll try every other line of enquiry we have. We won't give up. We'll find your daughter."

"Yes," Mr Jones added, "but will you find her in time? From what she said on the tape, we've got less than twenty four hours to track her down."

CHAPTER 9

Smithers picked up the scattered newspapers, and tossed them back into the wardrobe. He sneered at Wendy who was still bound and gagged. "So you know everything about me now, do you? Well, maybe you do, and maybe you don't."

'I know enough,' Wendy thought.

"Of course newspapers don't tell it all. There are lots of things they never find out. No-one ever knew what happened to some of my friends."

Smithers began to laugh. Wendy shivered. What had happened to his 'friends'? She had a horrible suspicion he was talking about other girls like herself. How many more had there been? How many had this man killed? And - she didn't like even to pose the question - what had he done to them before they died?

It was as if Smithers knew what she was thinking. "I'll look after you, little Wendy," he said, his voice suddenly gentle. He sat down on the bed beside her. "If you let me, I could be good to you. And I might change my mind about what I'll do with you..."

He stared at Wendy's eyes. Wendy wondered if he was looking to see if she believed him. But she wasn't fooled for a minute by his words. After holding her prisoner, beating her senseless, and allowing her to discover he had killed others, Smithers was not going to set her free. Whatever he said, he would never let her go. Wendy tried to return his stare, but found she couldn't. She turned her head away.

"Don't be like that," came Smithers' voice, quiet and pleading. "You've misunderstood me. I'm not bad, and I don't do cruel things. I like you, and want to be your friend." It was as if his personality had switched again to the kind, caring person she'd met originally at the cafe. "All I ever wanted to do was help you. You need someone to take care of you. I can do that, Wendy. Trust me..."

'I wouldn't trust you as far as I could throw you,' Wendy thought to herself.

"You don't need to be afraid of me," Smithers went on. He reached forward and pulled at the gag which was over Wendy's mouth. "Let me take this off," he said, as he eased apart a knot, and pulled the rag away from her face. "There, that's better, isn't it?"

Wendy thought about spitting in his face, but didn't. She would try being pleasant to this man. It could give her a chance. At least it might save her from more of his blows. She lay quietly, saying nothing.

Smithers' hand didn't move away from Wendy's face. He stroked her hair. "That's nice, now. See, I am good to you. You really like me, I know you do."

'You know nothing,' Wendy thought deep inside, hating every stroke of his hand.

His fingers moved softly over her forehead, then lightly through her hair again. Several minutes passed, and Wendy's tension began to ease. It didn't look as if Smithers was going to hurt her. She didn't like him touching, but he wasn't doing her any harm. The back of his hand brushed across her forehead again, and lingered for a moment on her cheek.

"Lie back, relax," he said soothingly. "Just enjoy it. It'll feel good."

For a moment Wendy almost did enjoy it. She was tired, and closed her eyes. She wanted to drift away into another world, a world of dreams and gentle experience. The hand that stroked her hair, and the fingers which caressed her face so tenderly, invited her to let go and allow her feelings to take control. She remembered how comforting it had been when she was really young, and she'd been frightened by a nightmare, to have her Dad sit on her bed and stroke her hair and ease her back to sleep. He had been really loving, really kind. This wasn't so different, was it?

A second later and Wendy was jolted out of her dream. Smithers' hand had moved down from her face to her neck. This wasn't what she wanted at all.

"No..." Wendy said firmly. Still tied, she couldn't pull herself away properly, but she managed to edge back an inch or two.

Smithers' voice stayed calm. "Don't worry. You're safe. I'm not doing anything bad," he said in a voice laced with innocence. He reached over and stroked Wendy's hair. "It's going to be all right, you'll see."

The gentle rhythm of his fingers began once more. Slowly, softly, he ran them down one side of her head, and then across and down the other. Sometimes he stayed quiet, sometimes he spoke in a whisper to her. "There," he said after Wendy seemed to have settled again, "you don't need to get hurt at all. There's just the two of us here. No-one will ever know what happens. It's much better when you do what I say." His hand stroked her hair, stroked her forehead, stroked her shoulder.

A moment later and she felt his hand move down her neck again. Every muscle in her body tensed. Another second, and the fingers were back stroking her hair. Then it was her neck, then his hand moved over her forehead. Carefully he touched her cheeks with the back of his fingers, and murmured quietly, "See, you like it. I know you like it. If you do what I want, I'll untie you."

Wendy didn't doubt for an instant what he meant. She said nothing, just stared at the wall. Smithers eased his fingers back through her hair, down to her shoulder, and then delicately over her neck. "Trust me," he said. "Everything will be fine."

His touch slowed, and Wendy sensed something else happening. It took only a second to recognise the tug on the top button of her blouse. 'Oh God no!' she said inside herself. 'Stop him somehow.'

The button came free. Wendy felt pressure build inside her. Her heart raced, her head hurt, and she was sure she would explode with fear and anger. Smithers' hand stroked her neck again. He pushed his fingers through her hair, ran them over her shoulder, and then reached back to her blouse. She felt him grope for the next button.

Quietly, invitingly, Wendy said, "Bill, just for a moment, stroke my face again please."

"Good," he said warmly. "You're enjoying it now. I knew you would." He moved his fingers slowly over her forehead. "There," he said. "That's nice isn't it?"

Wendy smiled at him. He smiled back. His fingers slipped down her cheeks, delicately brushing her skin. He caressed her face with the lightest touch, then ran the back of his hand over her lips, softly, gently.

It was the moment she'd wanted. Wendy's mouth parted, and her teeth sank hard and deep into Smithers' hand. She bit as if she wanted to tear his hand apart.

Smithers yelled in pain, and wrenched his hand clear. Blood immediately poured from the wound. "You bitch! You ungrateful bitch!" he yelled.

Wendy had a second in which to feel satisfied that she'd fought back before a mighty fist crashed against her head, and she sank into an unconsciousness that felt none of the other blows that rained down on her body.

* * * * *

The incident room at the police station buzzed with activity. Every officer had been called back on duty. They stood in small groups, some discussing the case and the new evidence which had come in, others complaining they'd lost a pleasant evening at home in front of the fire.

"Let me have your attention," Inspector Wilson called from the far end of the room. Heads turned in his direction, and a hush descended. "Right," said the Inspector, clutching a sheaf of papers, "I know none of you wants to be here tonight. But you'd better get used to it because I don't think any of you will be seeing your beds."

A few eyes rolled skyward, but before anyone could voice his moans, the Inspector added, "If you feel like complaining, remember there's a fifteen-year-old girl who isn't where she wants to be either, and if we don't find her she may never get the chance to see her home again."

No-one could argue with that statement. The police-men and women seemed to settle down, and listened carefully as assignments were handed out. Some would re-check records of past investigations into the disappearances of young girls, this time looking for the name Bill to crop up. Most were being dispatched to re-interview all their local contacts, to ask if the new name meant anything to them.

"Alright, are there any questions?" Inspector Wilson asked as he rounded off his briefing. There was silence. "No? Okay, let's get on with it. And I want to know anything you find out before you've even found it out, if you get my meaning."

Five minutes later, and two thirds of the police officers had dispersed. Most of those who stayed got busy on telephones or scanning computer records.

The Inspector stood with his hands on his hips surveying the scene. "If this girl is to have any chance at all, we'd better come up with something tonight," he said quietly.

* * * * *

A scruffy toothless cat was curled contentedly in Helen's lap. A saucer of milk and scraps of meat had seemed like a banquet to a cat which hadn't eaten for two days. Gappy had a new name now. Because of the tape which had been tied round his neck, Helen had decided to call him Abba. "You may not be pretty, Abba, but I'll look after you," she said. Gappy didn't care what he was called. He'd had plenty of names before, and Abba was as good as any of them. Anyway, now that he'd eaten, the sole item on his agenda was sleep.

The loud ringing of the phone nearly disturbed him, but only one ear stirred and he soon put that back in place.

107

Mrs Shaw answered the call.

"It's for you Helen," she said. "Don't worry, I'll bring the phone to you. I don't think that cat would appreciate you moving."

"Who's phoning me at this time?" asked Helen curiously.

"There's one sure way of finding out," her mother said, urging her to take the phone. "It's maybe the man of your dreams..."

Helen grasped the phone quickly, hoping the caller hadn't heard that last remark. "Hello..."

"Hi Helen, it's Fred," came a cheery voice.

"Hello *Fred*," said Helen, emphasising his name so that her mother's curiosity would be satisfied. "Is everything okay?"

"Yes, it's fine. I called because I've had the police at my home just now asking some more questions, and especially if I know someone called Bill. Do you know what this is all about?"

"I guess so," Helen said. She explained about the walk with her father, falling over the cat, and finding the tape.

Fred listened carefully. *"They didn't tell me all of that,"* he said once she'd finished. *"All I knew was that they were now looking for someone called Bill, and they wanted to know if there was anyone I could think of by that name that Wendy might have gone to."*

"And is there?" asked Helen anxiously.

"No, no-one at all. Sure, there are a few guys at school called Bill, and I told the police that. But I doubt if Wendy even knows them."

"I think the police will still check."

"Probably. They don't want to miss any lead."

"I wish I could come up with some ideas myself," Helen sighed. "I keep racking my brains, but I don't know a single person called Bill."

"This person could be a complete stranger, and that's what's making the hunt for him so difficult. Maybe Wendy didn't know him, and if she didn't, then probably none of us do either."

"That makes sense," said Helen.

"What I've also been thinking," Fred went on, *"is that we could be trying to answer the wrong question. Maybe we shouldn't keep asking who Wendy would go to, but where would she go? Perhaps she didn't know anyone in particular she'd want to run to. But she couldn't walk the streets forever. So where would she have gone?"*

"Have you any answers, Fred?"

"No, not yet. But it seems like that's the right question. Think about it, Helen. You're closer to Wendy than anyone."

"I'll try. Thanks Fred."

Helen put down the phone. She stroked the cat's ears, and a gentle purring indicated her affection was appreciated. "Where would Wendy go? Where indeed?" Helen asked quietly.

* * * * *

"Where am I...?" croaked Wendy's voice.

The small figure lay shrouded in darkness on the bed. Her head swam with pain and confusion as she struggled towards consciousness. Wendy's eyes couldn't seem to focus. She screwed them tight, and opened them again, but it made little difference. She tried to stretch to ease her cramp, but found it impossible. Tight rope still bound her hands and feet.

"What happened...?" she murmured, and then the memory began to form. Smithers... his hand... her retaliation... his vengeance. It seemed like a dream but the second she tried to move the shooting pains in her head told her it wasn't. Wendy wished she hadn't wakened.

She couldn't know how long she'd been unconscious. She guessed it had to be the middle of the night now, since there was virtually no light at all in the room. Her aching eyes could not even see the far wall, never mind read the time from the clock.

There was no way to know what had happened after she'd bitten Smithers' hand. She had a dull recollection of seeing his fist about to strike but remembered nothing after that. New hurts from several parts of her body told her Smithers had taken his revenge. Her cheek ached, and she could taste blood, so she guessed he'd targeted her face with many of his punches. 'I must look a real mess,' Wendy groaned.

She wondered where Smithers was now, and how much damage she'd done to his hand. She could not have inflicted serious injury, just enough to stop him molesting her. 'Enough that time,' she reckoned. 'But I'll never stop him if he tries again.' She hoped he was asleep downstairs.

The fog which imprisoned Wendy's mind to her surroundings suddenly lifted, and thoughts of her parents, of Helen, of what life was usually like rushed in. Her imagination awoke and she pictured what the last few days *should* have been like. She saw herself coming home from drama rehearsal, chatting to Mum while the meal was made, listening to some music until her Dad came in, and then the three of them sitting down to eat, and after that stretching out on her bed, watching whatever was on TV. She visualised the next morning, meeting up with Helen on the way to school, enjoying some lessons and enduring others, having a laugh with friends during the lunch break, and then longing for the afternoon to pass quickly. She pictured Dad in one of his crazy but good moods, phoning Mum and telling her not to bother making a meal. Instead she saw them going to a restaurant and on to watch a film at the cinema.

She had begun to invent the next day when a cold chill swept over Wendy, abruptly ending the pleasant thoughts. Lying in darkness, the contrast between what she had just imagined and what she was experiencing was all too great. 'None of that was real,' a small voice inside her head told her. 'None of those things happened. And they never will again!'

"Shut up!" Wendy almost shouted, even though she was talking to a voice which was inside her own mind.

'Your Dad has left. He doesn't care any more about your mother or about you. If he cared, he wouldn't have gone, would he?'

Wendy didn't want to hear that. It wasn't true. It couldn't be true. She didn't want it to be true.

'Everyone has forgotten you by now. Tonight your Dad was with his girlfriend, your Mum visited her own friends, and Helen was at home with her parents, getting on with her homework. You're history to them.'

'Surely that can't be true?' Wendy thought. 'They couldn't just forget me. They couldn't just leave me here?'

'No-one knows where you are, and no-one is coming to save you,' the voice went on relentlessly, brushing aside any faint hopes Wendy had. 'The only person you'll ever see again is Smithers...'

"No! I won't accept that!" Wendy said loudly. But what if the voice was right? She'd made sure she'd left no clues about where she was going. Since then there had been just two chances for anyone to find her. But she had not been quick enough to get Helen's and Fred's attention, and Helen and her father had come at the wrong time, and been reassured she wasn't there. None of them would be back.

Tears filled Wendy's sore eyes. The blackness of the night was nothing compared to the blackness she felt deep inside. She struggled to reawaken her imagination and remember the good times at home again, but now the thoughts only tortured her. She'd had so much, and thrown it all away. One stupid idea; one crazy gesture; and now she was tied up, starving, beaten, and going to die. Deep sobs shook her body, every one a small explosion of pain. But Wendy had given up caring. What did anything matter now?

CHAPTER 10

"It won't work," Mr Shaw said, frowning at his daughter.

"Why not? I think it's a brilliant plan," asserted Helen confidently, quite unaware of her lack of modesty.

They were sitting together at the breakfast table, with Mrs Shaw removing empty cereal bowls and replacing them with plates of toast and marmalade.

"Let me get this clear then..." Mr Shaw paused, trying to summarise the plan Helen had poured out in a torrent of words. "You'll take the cat back to the area of town where we found it, let it go, and hope to follow it to find Wendy."

"That's right," Helen enthused. "I was wishing last night that there was someone who had seen Wendy. But there was no-one, or so it seemed. Then I woke up early this morning and thought about the cat. He saw her. He knows where she is. He couldn't have had the tape tied round his neck if he hadn't come from wherever Wendy is held prisoner."

"I can't argue with that," said Mr Shaw. "But I don't think he'll go back there with you following."

"Why not?" Helen demanded.

"For one thing, cats never do what you want. But, even if he did cooperate with your plan, have you ever tried following a cat? Cats move fast when they want to.

You'd never keep up."

"I can run quickly."

"I've seen her in the school races," Mrs Shaw joined in. "Helen's a good runner."

Mr Shaw was unmoved. "There's all the difference between a quick hundred metre sprint on the athletics track and trying to pursue a cat through streets. Besides, no cat is going to stick to the main routes. He'll be off through back gardens, down small alleys, over fences... places you can't follow."

There was silence for a moment. Mr Shaw sipped his coffee quietly, wishing he could say something more positive to encourage his daughter.

"I've got it!" Helen said, her face brightening.

Her father's eyes rolled heavenward. "Tell me..."

"I'll put the cat on a lead, and then he can't escape from me. I'll feel which way he's tugging, and let him go slowly in that direction."

"That sounds incredibly silly to me," said Mr Shaw, and then regretted being so abrupt as he saw disappointment sweep over Helen's face.

"It *could* work, couldn't it?" Mrs Shaw said, trying to help.

"Look, I don't want to spoil a good idea," said Mr Shaw. "It's great that you're having ideas, but this one won't work. You can't pretend the cat is a St Bernard dog in the mountains, trained and ready to lead you to the person who needs rescue." He glanced at his watch. "I must go, or I'll be late for work. Helen, I don't think this is right. Don't try it."

Helen stared down at her toast, and said nothing. She felt her father pat her gently on the shoulder, and her mother followed him out to the front door to wave good-bye.

114

He was wrong this time. Helen knew it. Her plan was a good one, even if there were some problems. She *had* to do something to find Wendy. Her Dad might not like this idea, but he'd have a different opinion when the cat led her straight to her friend.

* * * * *

A creak on the stairs stirred Wendy's semi-consciousness better than any alarm clock had ever achieved. Smithers was coming, and her frail, hurting body tensed at the thought. The utter darkness of the night had passed, and tiny shafts of light crept round the boards which had been nailed over the window. With them came the dread of new and ever more frightening experiences.

'What will happen this time? What will he do?' Wendy wondered, the questions terrifying her. Her wrists and ankles were still tied, and she felt vulnerable. At least he would keep his hands away from her face.

The key was turned in the lock, and the door opened. Smithers was silhouetted against the light from the hallway outside. He stood still, looking at her silently for a moment, and then sauntered in and flung a newspaper on the bed. "You're big news," he said, walking over towards the window to check that the wood was secure.

Wendy screwed her head round to try and see the front page of the paper. It was awkward, but she managed to read the main headline, FEARS MOUNT FOR MISSING GIRL. Alongside was her photograph. It was one of the portraits her parents insisted were taken of her every two years when a photographer visited the school. She had never liked any of them, including this one. It made her look much more formal than she cared to be.

"They'll find me," she said to Smithers.

"Yes, they'll do that," he replied, turning back in her direction. "But they'll find you only when I'm ready, and you won't know anything about it." His face creased as he gave an evil chuckle. "I'm not sure yet where I'll put your body. Maybe a ditch. Maybe in a pond. Maybe I'll leave it in your parents' garden, now that the paper has told me your address."

"You're sick!" Wendy said fiercely.

Smithers laughed. "I've heard that before, but I don't care what you say. In fact, after last night I don't care for you at all. I had thought you might have your uses..." He sat on the end of the bed, and laid his hand on Wendy's leg. She winced, and drew her legs off to one side, away from his reach. "See, you're just an ungrateful little girl. And," he snarled, "I'm angry with you."

Fear surged inside Wendy. This cruel man could do anything he wanted with her, and she wouldn't be able to stop him. She felt tears in her eyes. Fighting for self-control, she said nothing, hoping he would just go away.

But Smithers didn't move. Instead he reached into a pocket, and pulled out a leather pouch from which he drew a long bladed knife. One edge was curved, and looked as though it had been sharpened over and over again. The top edge was serrated and would rip anything to bits. Wendy held her breath. She had seen knives like it in anglers' stores. She shuddered to see one in this man's hand.

Smithers turned the knife back and forward, playing with the blade. He looked up at Wendy, watching for her reaction. She tried to stare back at him, but after a few moments she had to look away.

"You've made me angry," he went on finally. "I

never wanted to be angry or disappointed with you. I thought you might be different from the others. But you're not. You're just as bad as they were. So you'll have to die. Tonight..."

Wendy closed her eyes, and tried to concentrate on something else - anything - so that she didn't have to listen to what he said. But the more she didn't want to hear, the more his words burned their way into her mind.

"We could have had a good friendship," he went on. "But you didn't want that. Instead you did this!" He turned his hand over, and thrust the back of it in front of Wendy's face. " Look what you did to me."

Wendy opened her eyes, and saw a red, fiery gash torn in the skin, with the marks of her teeth still showing clearly.

"I should have killed you last night for that," Smithers said. "Maybe that would have been wise... Because it's not just your stupid and pointless attack that's making me angry." He grabbed the paper, and held the front page up for Wendy to see properly. Her eyes quickly took in the picture and the main heading again, and she began to read the article. 'Police are stepping up their search for 15-year-old Wendy Jones following her disappearance on Thursday...'

"Don't read that," Smithers said impatiently. "Try this." His finger pointed to the small box near the side of the paper in which they printed late news. Under a tiny heading of 'Wendy Jones search', the article stated, 'Midnight news: Police hunting for Wendy Jones have said they want to interview a man by the name of Bill in connection with their enquiries. Anyone with information is urged to come forward." Before she could read any more, he snatched the paper away.

"Now how do you suppose they got my name?" he quizzed. He laid the knife blade against Wendy's leg menacingly. "Could some little bird here have somehow got a message out...?"

Wendy felt the knife begin to press harder against her, but fear became submerged beneath a tremor of hope. Her tape had got to someone! Courage rose in her, and she looked straight at Smithers. "They'll find me," she said. "I've told you that. And they'll catch you."

"Not a chance."

"Yes they will. You're not going to kill me. God is on my side."

"God? *God!?* Now I could have thought a lot of things about you, but never that I'd hear you say that. Don't make me laugh."

"Well he is," Wendy found herself saying, almost to her own surprise. "And he's looking after me."

"Then he's not making too good a job of it until now," Smithers said. "You should see yourself. In fact, I think I'll let you do that." He stood up, and left the room. Wendy was glad the knife was gone for the moment with him. But a second later he was back, a small mirror in his hand.

"Now take a look at yourself," he said, holding the mirror a short distance away from her.

Wendy couldn't believe that the face staring back from the mirror was her. Hollow, blackened eyes peered from beneath matted, tangled hair. The cheeks were swollen and mouth cut, with streaks of dried blood and dark bruises providing the only colour. The face looked as though it belonged to a war refugee. Could this really be her just two days after leaving home?

Smithers laughed as he saw how shocked Wendy was

at her own reflection. "Not so pretty now, are you?" he said cruelly. He propped up the mirror on the bedside cabinet. "I'll put this here, so you can look at yourself every now and again. After all, it'll be the last chance you have to admire yourself..."

With another sneering chuckle, Smithers backed away.

"Are you going to leave me tied up like this all day?" Wendy asked. "These ropes hurt."

"Shame, isn't it? But this way you won't be ripping panels away from the window or sending anyone messages. When you're tied up, I feel a lot more secure. You won't be going anywhere while I'm out."

Wendy buried her face in the pillow. She was so frightened she wanted to cry, but she wouldn't let this evil man see that.

Because she wasn't looking, it was without warning that she suddenly found herself pinned to the bed. Smithers' knee pressed into her back, and she felt something pulled round her neck. For one terrifying moment she thought he was going to strangle her. Then a tug at her mouth made her realise Smithers was replacing the gag. He jerked her head back, pulled the rag into place, knotted it as tight as he could, and then flung her head back on to the pillow.

"I wouldn't like you to do any shouting if anyone happened to walk past, not that they will. Now, enjoy your final day," Smithers said. "You've got until 7 o'clock..." He moved towards the door, then paused and looked down at his watch. "Just ten hours to live." He laughed as if that was the funniest fact in the world. Then he pulled the door behind him, and left.

* * * * *

It hadn't been easy to persuade the toothless cat that he ought to have a length of string tied round his neck. Helen had several scratches on her hands to prove how unwilling Abba had been. But finally she'd got it fastened, and crept out of the house without her mother knowing.

Helen walked far enough up the lane from her house to be certain she wouldn't be seen. She laid the cat on the ground, making sure she had a tight hold on the end of the string. "Right," she informed Abba. "Let's go. We're off back to town, and then you're going to lead me to where Wendy is."

The cat stretched each paw in turn, like an athlete preparing for the big race. Helen felt encouraged. This would be easier than she'd thought. How wrong her father had been. Abba lifted his nose, sniffed the air, bent his back low, and promptly sat down. A moment later his head was between his paws, and his eyes were closing for a mid-morning snooze.

"That's not the idea," Helen protested, giving the string a sharp tug. "We're meant to be finding Wendy." She pulled hard enough to force Abba back to his feet, but the cat had no intention of going anywhere Helen wanted. When she pointed him forward, he moved sideways. When she pushed him back on course, he turned right round and made for the house. When she corrected that, he sat down again.

"This is hopeless!" Helen said, exasperated. "I'll be kind to you, Abba, and assume you simply don't know where you are." She picked him up. "Come on. I'll carry you until we get to town, and maybe then - when you see your surroundings - you'll walk sensibly."

Abba seemed very happy to be carried. Helen strode briskly down the rest of the lane, and then followed the road which eventually took her to the town centre. Quite a few people turned their heads for a second look at this girl with a cat in her arms. Helen felt embarrassed and avoided returning their glances. Abba didn't mind though, and gave every onlooker a toothless grin.

Finally, Helen reached the street where she'd tripped over Abba the previous evening. That was the area in which to start the search. Abba had to have a home somewhere, she reckoned, even if it was only a shed where he slept. Now that he was back on familiar ground, he'd want to go there sooner or later. She'd follow him, and that just might lead her to Wendy. With time running out, it was worth a try.

Abba jumped out of her arms as soon as she bent down with him. Helen had to grasp the end of her string quickly, or he might have dashed off without her. "Hold on a second," she told him quickly. "I'm coming with you wherever you go." She gave a gentle tug on the string to let Abba know she was there.

That was the signal for Abba to go on strike again. He curled his head round and up to look at Helen, as if to say, 'And who do you think you are to put me on a lead?' Then he slunk down, rolled on his back, pawed playfully at the string for a moment, and showed not the slightest interest in moving.

"Come on," Helen said, trying another tug. But Abba had found a pool of sunshine, and seemed to have settled to get as much of a tan as a black cat could.

"Oh! You unhelpful cat!" Helen complained. "Don't you want to find my friend? Don't you know her life could depend on you?" But Abba's conscience was untroubled, and he displayed no inclination to stir and take Helen anywhere. It seemed her father was right, and

121

this idea would never work.

'I'll make it work,' Helen told herself almost angrily. 'I *know* this is the way to find Wendy.' With a new determination, she crouched down and undid the knot holding the string around the cat's neck. She could follow Abba, string or no string.

"Now, you're free. Let's get going!" said Helen.

Abba seemed to take the hint. Getting rid of his noose made all the difference. Slowly he stood, stretching each leg in turn. His nose sniffed the air. Helen hoped he was getting a sense of direction.

A second later he was off. Helen was almost too late as the cat disappeared between a forest of pedestrians' legs, but Abba was only strolling gently, and it wasn't hard to keep up. He sauntered down the pavement, pausing occasionally near some shop doorway as if to check what might be of interest for him inside. A counter laden with fish was almost too much of a distraction, but Helen chased Abba on. This was no time for him to be thinking of his stomach.

Weaving in and out between people, Abba made steady progress. Round one bend, then another, he strolled, Helen never far behind. Her hopes rose. Abba was going somewhere, and it might be back to wherever he'd met Wendy.

But then he stopped. For no reason Helen could see, Abba suddenly halted and sat down. Helen held back, not wanting to disturb him, sure he'd move again in a moment. Abba, however, had decided it was time for a wash. He lifted his paw, licked it with his long tongue, and proceeded to clean thoroughly behind his ears. The noise of traffic and the scurrying past of pedestrians didn't seem to bother him in the slightest. After all, personal hygiene deserved time.

Anxiety mounted inside Helen. Abba might be in no hurry, but she was. Every minute that went past was another in which Wendy was in terrible danger. For all she knew, whoever was planning Wendy's death might be about to carry out his threat. It simply wouldn't do for Abba to sit in the sunshine and wash his matted fur. He had to be hurried on. She'd count to ten, and if he didn't move, she'd make him move.

"One, two, three," Helen counted softly. She was standing a couple of paces away in a shop doorway, watching carefully. "Four, five, six, seven..." Abba seemed thoroughly content. "If only he'd get going," she sighed. If Abba chose to walk on himself, he'd head in a direction he wanted. If she intervened, he might take just any route, and not one which led to Wendy. But... "Eight, nine..." She waited. Still the cat licked his paw and washed his fur. "Right, *ten*," Helen said forcefully.

She stepped out from her doorway, walked quietly up behind Abba, and then loudly clapped her hands to startle him.

The cat jumped. Abba didn't even glance back to see where the noise had come from, but shot forward straight over the road. Brakes squealed and tyres screeched, followed by a horrible thud. Helen screamed as she saw a black ball of fur thrown through the air.

CHAPTER 11

Inspector Wilson looked up hopefully as his sergeant entered the room. "Any developments?" he asked.

"I'm not sure," Sergeant Turner replied wearily, slumping in a chair. Both men were feeling the strain of this investigation. Neither had gone home the previous night, and a couple of hours dozing in a chair had given little real rest.

The Inspector sensed the man's hesitation, and was too tired to be patient. "But have you got *something?*" he asked bluntly.

The sergeant held up a fax message which had just arrived. "It's from one of the forces to the south. We asked everyone to check their records for anyone called 'Bill' who was suspected of assaults on young girls. This report is the only one which has come back positive. Our lads there had questioned a man called Bill Smithers after a couple of disappearances."

"What came of the investigations?"

"Not a lot," it seems. "There were a few circumstantial details to associate Smithers with the disappearances, but nothing in the way of hard evidence. So they couldn't press any charges against him. He was never brought to any trial. Mind you, neither was anyone else in those cases, so he remains a suspect even now."

"And is he still on their patch?"

"No, that's what makes him a little more interesting to us. He's gone. Somewhere further north is all that our boys were told when they tried to trace him. They're not happy about losing touch with him, and our enquiry has made them wonder if he could have moved into our area. They'd like to find out..."

"Not half as much as I would," said Wilson forcefully. "It may be a long shot, but we're looking for someone called 'Bill' who's got a girl from our area, and at the same time the boys down south have lost a Bill Smithers who may have a track record with girls. It could be just a coincidence. But there's a chance he's come here, and Wendy Jones has disappeared because of him." The Inspector stood up, stretching his limbs. Something tangible to work on was bringing a little energy back into his bones. "Do we have a photo?"

"They're sending one on in the next hour. We already have a description." The sergeant scanned the sheet before him. "He's twenty, about five feet ten inches, sandy brown hair, pale complexion, slightly bent nose, slim build."

"Okay, let's circulate his name and details among all our people now, and get them working on checking hotels, guest houses, and estate agents to see if anyone has let a room or property to Smithers or anyone matching his description."

Turner looked at his watch. "From what the tape said, we have only today." He hesitated. "Maybe nine hours...? Can we possibly get anything in time?"

Inspector Wilson closed his eyes for a moment. There was an enormous temptation to give in to the difficulty of it all. But a young girl's life depended on none of them giving up. "We'll never know if there was time unless we try," he said. "We've got to do our best."

* * * * *

Helen sat in the kitchen at home, refusing to be comforted by her mother. "It's alright, dear," Mrs. Shaw said. "You weren't to know that the cat would run across the road."

"I *should* have known. I *should* have guessed," Helen spluttered, struggling to get the words out between sobs.

"Well, you wanted to try out your idea..."

"Yes, but I didn't want to get Abba killed." Helen stood up, wiping tears away from her eyes. She looked at her mother's concerned face. "And how am I ever going to explain to Dad? He told me not to try following the cat."

Mrs Shaw raised her eyebrows. It wasn't often that Helen went directly against her father's wishes. "I'm sure he'll do his best to understand. He'll know you were really worried about Wendy."

"I hope so," said Helen.

Mrs Shaw filled the kettle with water. It was time for a cup of tea. "What have you done with the cat's body?" she asked, being practical.

"I haven't done anything," Helen confessed. "After the accident I screamed and screamed, and then ran away. I couldn't look at Abba lying dead in the road." There was a long pause before Helen continued. "After ten minutes, though, I went back. But there was no Abba. Someone must have taken his body away."

Her mother thought for a moment, and then said "Or

- and I know this is not likely - he might have been so injured he crawled off. I've heard of animals doing that. It seems they want to be alone to die."

"But then he might be in pain, just lying somewhere by himself... Oh, that's terrible," Helen said, and began to cry again.

"Come on now, Helen. You can't torture yourself like that. Abba won't have suffered. I'm sure he'll have been in a state of shock, and probably just 'fallen asleep', if you understand what I mean."

Helen understood exactly what her mother meant. But if the cat had survived the impact she wasn't at all sure he would have died peacefully. Mrs Shaw guessed she hadn't convinced Helen. "If you want, you can go out again later, and check that he's not lying injured somewhere."

Helen calmed down. "And if I find his body, I can bring him home and we'll give him a decent burial."

Mrs Shaw nodded. She could believe her daughter would do that.

* * * * *

Wendy was getting more and more despondent that there was nothing she could do to save herself. She couldn't bear the thought of just lying on that bed waiting for Smithers to come back and kill her. There had to be a way to escape this room which had become her condemned cell. But how? She was locked behind a door she could never break down, the window boarded up with planks of wood, and she was tied and gagged. She was weak with hunger, her face swollen, her side aching with the slightest movement, and she hurt in several other places too

127

from the beatings she'd had. The little hope she had once had was withering.

'Come on, Wendy, admit it. You're as good as dead now,' said a small voice in her head. Wendy didn't want to listen, but the voice wouldn't stop. 'You blew it when you ran off from home, and made it worse when you trusted a man like Smithers.' Wendy knew that the voice was speaking the truth. 'And now you're getting what you deserve, not just for running off but for all the wrong things you've done.'

The pain in her head seemed to increase as the voice droned on and on, accusing her of being a failure in almost every area of life, and telling her the situation was hopeless now. If Wendy could have freed her hands she'd have put them tight over her ears, but it would have made little difference. How do you shut out a voice that is coming from deep inside? 'You've got to be realistic now, Wendy.' The voice appeared to be drawing her to an inevitable conclusion. 'Everyone else has given up on you. Your family don't love you, your friends have abandoned you, and God doesn't care. You've nothing to hope for now. You might as well give up trying, give up on life, give up on God.'

Tears began to form in Wendy's eyes. She'd never felt so alone as at that moment. Her Dad didn't love her, nor her Mum. They couldn't, not now she'd run away. Helen...? Probably Helen would miss her, but only for a short time. Helen was a popular girl. She'd soon find another friend. And God? For a while she'd thought God really was going to help her. But nothing had happened. He didn't care either. The voice was right, and she might as well give up trying, give up on life, and give up on God. Wendy let the tears come, and they rolled down her face uncontrolled since there was nothing she could do to wipe them away.

Some minutes later the tears and sobs ceased, and Wendy stretched to try and ease her discomfort. She rolled over, the movement sending stabs of pain across her side before she settled again on the grubby bed. She felt a prisoner, a prisoner of that dingy room and a prisoner of an ever darkening despair. There was nothing to hope for now. So the voice had said. And the voice told the truth.

'No it doesn't,' came another unexpected voice deep inside Wendy's thoughts. This one spoke with great authority. 'There *is* hope. My plans are to give you hope and a future.' Wendy recognised those words immediately. It was part of the Bible verse from the newspaper. 'For I know the plans I have for you, plans to prosper you and not to harm you, plans to give you hope and a future.' The voice inside her head recited the promise back to her again, and in that moment Wendy felt an absolute certainty that it was right. *This* was the truth.

Could God be speaking to her? The idea seemed silly. God didn't utter words into thin air. Yet, what she was 'hearing' wasn't some loud voice from a corner of the room. It was as if she simply knew what God was saying deep inside herself. She couldn't understand how that could happen, or why God would bother with her. But this was not the moment for those questions. What mattered was that God had not abandoned her, and she knew she would escape. Escape was impossible, but more than once Helen had told her that God was the God of the impossible. At last Wendy felt again that there was something worth living for. If she could have, she would have smiled.

Wendy did something she had never done before. She prayed. Because of the gag on her mouth, the words had to be spoken inside her mind. But this was a real prayer, not something she'd read in any book, but exactly what she wanted to say to God at that moment. *"Dear God, thank you for not giving up on me. Thank you for giving me hope. I believe you mean me to live. Show me how. Please show me how."* Wendy hesitated, and then added, *"So here's my life. I give it to you. Now whether I live or die, it's yours to do with as you want."* That was it. Wendy had nothing else to say, so she stopped.

She was still tied up, the door was still locked and the window barred. Wendy was as much a prisoner as before. Yet, sensing her life was in God's hands, she had never felt more free.

* * * * *

Wendy's parents slumped in their chairs, eyes bleary with tiredness, heads sore with worry and lack of sleep. Each seemed to stare into a different corner of the room, lost in a world of thought which could not be shared at that moment. Terrifying fears danced through their minds, as their imaginations pictured their daughter held prisoner. What kind of madman had her? What had he done to hurt her already? What would he do in just a few hours? The questions were enemies. Both wanted to fight them off or shut them out, but they advanced relentlessly. They would not be resisted, and minute by minute inflicted ever greater wounds of despair.

The phone rang, and the couple stirred. "I'll get it," said Mr Jones with no great enthusiasm. It must have been the hundredth call in the last twenty four hours.

Time after time they had leapt to answer, thinking it might be someone with good news for them, or even Wendy to say she was free. But after fifty, sixty, and then seventy times of being disappointed, they'd stopped hoping. They were grateful that friends phoned to wish them well, and they tolerated the reporters who wanted to know of any new developments, since publicity might help in tracing Wendy. Yet, no matter how large the headlines or how heart-rending the TV reports, so far press coverage had changed nothing. Their daughter was still lost, and they were no nearer knowing where to look for her.

Mrs Jones settled back into her chair, staring across at the far wall, almost oblivious to her husband's voice talking on and off in the background. Eventually he finished and took his seat again.

"That was Mrs Shaw, Helen's mother," he said quietly.

"Good of her to call," said Mrs Jones in a tired voice and without moving her eyes. "I don't suppose she has any news?"

"No, she hasn't. She just wanted us to know she was thinking of us, and praying for us as well as for Wendy."

This time Mrs Jones didn't reply, and the words were allowed to hang in the air.

"Maybe..." Mr Jones began slowly a few minutes later. "Maybe we should think about praying as well?" The words came tentatively, Mr Jones almost surprising himself that he was suggesting it.

He certainly got his wife's attention. She looked up sharply at her husband, wondering if the strain of these last two days had finally made him break down. But the look on his face told her he was absolutely serious. "Pray?"

she said after a moment. "We've never prayed before."

"Maybe it's time we started," said Mr Jones with a growing authority in his voice. "If someone else can pray for us and our daughter, surely we ought to do some praying ourselves."

"I didn't even know you believed in God."

"I always have... Well, sort of. It's just that I've never done much about it. There's never seemed to be time to fit God in. I've always been doing other things."

"Too many other things..." his wife said dryly.

"Okay, too many other things, and too many of them wrong things. But they're not the issue now. Our daughter is what matters, and if there's a God he knows where she is, and if there's a God who has any power and any love he can help her. We should ask."

Mrs Jones sat thinking, and her husband grew quiet as well. For several minutes neither moved. Only the tick of the clock on the wall broke the silence.

"I don't know how to pray," Mrs Jones said eventually. "I've often wanted to, but I don't know how to start." It sounded like a confession.

"Presumably you just tell God what you want to tell him," said Mr Jones.

"That's too simple. Church people use long and complicated sentences, and special words. That must be how you're meant to talk to God."

Mr Jones allowed himself to think. "I can't believe the vocabulary you use makes any difference," he said after a while. "God understands plain speaking, and I don't think he's going to hold it against us if we miss out on the jargon."

"Well, we'll have to kneel. People always kneel to pray."

"Do they? What difference does it make if you stand, sit, kneel or lie down, as long as you actually pray?"

"I don't know, but we're going to have to kneel," said Mrs Jones emphatically. "If we're doing this, we'd better do it properly."

"I'm sure it won't improve the prayer, but if it matters to you, I'll kneel." More forcefully than ever, Mr Jones added, "I think the most important thing now is that we get on and do it."

He slipped from his chair to his knees. Mrs Jones sighed, and knelt beside him on the fireside rug. Mr Jones closed his eyes. Mrs Jones wasn't quite so quick. She snatched a glance over her shoulder to check no-one was looking through the window. Thankfully all was quiet. She closed her eyes as well. A second later she felt her hand taken gently, even tenderly. It hadn't happened for years. On their knees, husband and wife were together again.

Two minutes slipped by, and then three. Neither had prayed. "I'm waiting for you," said Mrs Jones finally.

"Oh!" came her husband's surprised voice. "I was waiting for you."

They opened their eyes, looked at each other, and smiled. It had been the first smile for a long time. "What a pair of embarrassed fools we are," said Mr Jones. "Okay, I'll pray."

Both closed their eyes again.

"*God,*" he began, and then stopped. He knew what he wanted to say, but it was hard to get the words out. A minute later he went on, "*God, I haven't paid you much attention. I suppose I've been too busy, and I just wanted to do the things that pleased me. I'm sorry...*" There was another pause, and Mr Jones seemed to be struggling to stop himself crying. *"I'm really sorry... I've messed up so much. Both of us have. God, if you can forgive, please forgive us. We want to get it right now. And we need help."* The words began to flow and speed up. *"Our daughter needs help. Maybe you're the only one who can save her now. Please - wherever she is - get her out. Don't let her die. Oh God, please don't let her die. Give her some way of escape. Whatever it takes, get her free. Please..."* With that the words came to an end.

Together they knelt a while longer, each adding some silent and private prayers. And, as best they could they made their own promises to God. After what seemed a long time, each sensed the other had finished. Mr Jones put his arms round his wife, pulled her close, and they held each other. At last they knew there was hope, for Wendy and for them.

* * * * *

The hand mirror that Smithers had left on the bedside cabinet lay at an angle that allowed Wendy to see herself. She groaned as she caught sight of her battered face in its reflection, and wondered if she would ever look right again. 'I don't suppose I should worry about being pretty, only about getting free,' she told herself.

The mirror! Suddenly Wendy's brain went into overdrive. The mirror! It was just what she needed. She knew exactly what she had to do to begin escaping from her death cell.

CHAPTER 12

Wendy would never escape as long as she was forced to lie tied up on the bed. She had to get rid of the rope round her wrists and ankles. That's where the mirror could help. There was only a slim chance, but if she could smash the mirror, she might be able to use one of the sharp edges of glass to cut through the rope.

Wendy pulled herself towards the bedside cabinet, wincing as pain grabbed at her side. She would have to ignore it as best she could if she was to get free. She pushed hard with her legs, dragging herself up the bed. It was far from easy, but after a few minutes she'd got her head and shoulders to the same height as the cabinet. A final struggle and she was in position. She needed to knock the mirror to the ground to break the glass. Wendy closed her eyes, and gave the mirror a neat sideways flick with her head that a footballer would have been proud of. There was a loud clatter as the mirror hit the ground.

Wendy looked down eagerly. 'Oh no...' she groaned. The mirror was still intact. The carpet had cushioned the fall, and the glass hadn't broken. It seemed unfair to Wendy. Usually things broke so easily, and now this mirror wouldn't smash when she wanted it to.

'What can I do now?' she wondered. For some minutes she lay still, working out another plan. Then she had it. She'd get down on the floor, wedge the mirror between her feet, do a backward somersault and launch the mirror against the wall. 'Brilliant! That'll smash it to bits,' she told herself, stifling thoughts of how difficult such a tumbling act might actually be.

Rolling off the bed was easy enough. Wendy swallowed down the shooting pains she felt from various parts of her body. It was hard to breathe because of the gag, and the effort of movement made that worse. But Wendy was not going to give up without a fight. She got herself into a seated position, and wriggled over the carpet until the mirror was beside her feet. With her ankles bound tightly, she had very little freedom to move either foot. She needed to be able to grip with them. During the previous day she had put on her shoes, and that would help. The mirror was lying face down on the carpet. With one foot she pushed down on the edge of the mirror's frame, sinking it into the carpet and causing the other edge to rise slightly. That was just enough to slip her other foot under it, and gently straighten the mirror into a vertical position, wedged now between both feet.

Wendy looked over her shoulder, as if to take aim. She drew as deep a breath as she could, hoped her feet had a good hold on the mirror, and threw herself backwards. It was awkward and sore rolling over her arms, but she gritted her teeth and made herself do it. Her legs flipped up, and Wendy let the mirror go to send it flying against the wall behind her. But she was a fraction too quick in releasing the mirror. Instead of being driven backwards, it flopped straight up in the air, and dropped intact back on to the carpet.

Wendy gasped for air. 'Try again...' she said silently, refusing to be beaten. She got the mirror back in position between her shoes, thought carefully what she was going to do, and then somersaulted backwards. This time she held on too long. Instead of flying against the wall, the mirror was neatly deposited on the floor behind Wendy's head. It was a trick her gymnastics teacher would have been proud of, but no use to Wendy at that moment.

'Come on, Wendy, you can do this,' she lectured herself, feeling angry that it was proving so difficult just to smash a mirror. She pulled herself round, and gathered the mirror securely between her feet again. 'Let's see if I can manage it in the other direction.' She worked it out. She'd roll back, flip her legs over, and release the mirror at exactly the midpoint so that it was thrown across the room to hit the opposite wall. This time it was going to work. She knew it.

She got ready, lined herself up, held her breath, and rolled... She moved faster than ever before, and was sure she'd let go of the mirror at the right moment and listened for the crash. It never came. All Wendy heard was another soft bump as the mirror landed somewhere, but she had no idea where.

Wendy unrolled forwards, and felt something crunch under her bottom. She drew her breath in sharply. The mirror! She'd come down on it! As carefully as she could she slid over to one side in case she did herself serious injury from sharp fragments of glass. But she was unhurt, and when she looked back, there lay the mirror now broken into pieces. Wendy tried to smile. 'All that rolling about, and all you have to do to smash a mirror is sit on it.'

With no time to waste, she examined the debris.

Some fragments were too small to be of any use, but several others were long razor-edged pieces, exactly what she needed.

Because her hands were tied behind her back, the next part would also be far from easy. Wendy struggled on to her knees, faced away from the broken mirror, and slithered about until she knew it was right behind her feet. She leaned back, fumbling with her fingers for the broken glass. A painful prick made her wince, and reinforced how sharp some of the edges of glass were. She would have to be careful. As cautiously as she could, she traced the outline of one of the long strands, and picked it up.

Now came the hard bit. Arching her back, Wendy pushed the glass into the small gap between her shoes. When it felt in place, she gripped hard with her feet, leaving a sharp edge sticking out. It would be her saw to cut through the rope.

Her hands were tied so tight, she would have to saw close to her wrists. That would have been dangerous at any time, but she would have to accomplish it without seeing what she was doing. Nervously she reached down, felt carefully from side to side with her hands to sense the glass's position, and then tried to press the rope against its edge. When she felt contact, she began a short sawing movement up and down to cut away at the rope.

Hope rose in Wendy. This really might work. A second later that hope vanished as the glass stabbed deeply into her wrist. A ball of pain shot through her, her eyes instantly filled with tears, and she nearly fainted.

Somehow she kept her balance, and eventually regained her senses. She bit tight on the gag over her mouth, fighting the pain that wanted to control her and make her give up. Near her hands she felt a trickle of blood. 'How much damage have I done to myself?' she wondered. She looked over her shoulder. She couldn't twist round far enough to see her wrists, but she could tell that blood wasn't spurting out. Her basic knowledge of first aid told her that meant she couldn't have severed an artery. Yet the cut seemed like a warning, and Wendy felt even more scared. 'If I stab myself badly, I could lose so much blood I'll die kneeling here on this carpet. Instead of Smithers killing me, I'll end up killing myself!' There were real risks in trying to get free.

She looked over at the clock. It was 12 o'clock. In just seven hours Smithers was coming back to murder her. There were even greater risks in not trying to get free.

* * * * *

"Alright, alright, I'm coming!" The doorbell wasn't usually pushed and held in for ten or fifteen seconds, and Mrs Shaw felt flustered as she made her way to the door.

She pulled open the front door. There stood Sergeant Turner and a uniformed constable beside him. "Good morning officers," Mrs Shaw stammered, surprised to find policemen calling again.

"Good *afternoon*," the sergeant corrected her.

"Oh yes, so it is," Mrs Shaw replied, looking at her watch and seeing it was nearly 12.30.

"Could we come in for a moment, please?" pressed the sergeant.

"Of course." Mrs Shaw opened the door wide and ushered the two men into the main room, where they sat on the couch.

"Is Helen here? She's the one we really want to see."

"No, I'm sorry, I'm afraid she went out fifteen minutes ago. You've just missed her. Perhaps I could help?"

"Do you know where Helen has gone, Mrs Shaw?"

139

"I'm not really sure, I'm afraid." Mrs Shaw sensed the officers' disapproval. "Oh, she's perfectly safe. I wouldn't have let her go off on her own at a time like this, but she phoned her friend Fred and arranged to meet up with him. They're looking for a dead cat which has wandered off."

The policemen exchanged glances with each other. "Dead cats don't usually wander off..." the constable began to say.

The sergeant sensed some unwise comment coming, so before the constable could go on he interrupted, "Mrs Shaw, we have a photograph here of a man who might be able to help us with our enquiries." He pulled a picture from a large folder he was carrying. "We wanted to show it to Helen in case she recognised him. But perhaps you would look at it for us."

Mrs Shaw took the photograph, and studied it carefully. She tilted it to the side, as if that might give her a different angle on the picture. But after a minute she shook her head. "I'm sorry. It doesn't look like anyone I know, except..." She paused, and the policemen leaned forward expectantly. "It is like a photo I have of my Uncle Frank when he was younger. But he's 85 now and in a home for the elderly."

The constable's shoulders began to heave gently, and his sergeant glanced across at him. The man was biting his lip fiercely. The thought that geriatric Uncle Frank could be their wanted man and the idea of a search party for a renegade dead cat seemed to be getting to him. The sergeant swallowed down a severe temptation to let the humour take him over as well.

"Well, thank you very much anyway, Mrs Shaw," he said quickly and replaced the photograph in the folder.

"Mr Shaw is not around, I presume?"

"No, I'm afraid he's having to work today."

"In that case, we won't detain you any longer. We're anxious to let Helen see this man's photograph, so when she returns perhaps you could get her to call us and we'll bring it out again or have her come down to the station."

"I'll certainly do that. So, has the man in the photograph got Wendy?"

"We don't know. But it's important that we find him as soon as possible. I'm sure you know the phrase - we have to 'eliminate him from our inquiries'."

Mrs Shaw nodded, and the two men got up to go. Mrs Shaw led them to the door. As they left, Sergeant Turner couldn't resist a final word. With great seriousness he said, "I do hope they track down the dead cat before it gets too far away." His colleague pushed past him, stuffing his handkerchief into his mouth as he went. A minute later the two men sat in their police car, uncontrollable tears of laughter streaming down their faces.

* * * * *

Uncontrollable tears of pain streamed down Wendy's face. She had knelt on the floor for more than two hours, and accidentally cut her wrists over and over again as she tried desperately to free herself. The agony was immense, greater than any pain she had known in her life. Now when she twisted round, she could see a red stain on the carpet which told her she had lost a great deal of blood. But she had to keep going. She had to try. To give up was to accept death when God had promised her life.

Back and forth she pushed the rope against the glass.

Countless times the fragment had slipped from between her shoes, and she'd had to stretch down and replace it. She'd almost mastered that technique, but when she began her sawing action again, she couldn't know if she was still cutting against the same bit of the rope, or starting on a new part each time. Would she ever succeed? It seemed impossible.

Wendy rested for a moment. Exhaustion was becoming almost as big a problem as the pain and weakness. When she thought about it she realised how little she had slept for the last three days and nights. She'd lain awake most of the night after her Dad's terrible announcement, and sleep had been minimal since coming into Smithers' house. A mixture of terror, pain, and discomfort had robbed her of any true rest. At most, her weary body had claimed sleep for an hour or two at a time, after which she'd wakened and lain shivering in the cold and terror of the darkness. Now energy simply wasn't there when she needed it. 'Did all this begin just three days ago?' she asked herself incredulously. It felt more like a month had passed.

Depressing though the thoughts were, she would not give in. Wendy stirred herself. 'I must do this. God, I must do this,' she said firmly to herself.

Her shoulders ached. Her hands had been tied behind her since the previous day, and now the stretching backwards to reach the glass made Wendy feel as if someone had put her shoulders between a giant vice which was slowly being closed and crushing her.

But on and on she went, pushing the rope as firmly against the sharp edge of glass as she dared. She knew that if the rope slipped and the dagger like fragment of mirror stabbed her once more, it could be fatal. 'Come on, come on, *come on...*' she chanted in her head in rhythm with the movement. "It must cut, it must cut, *it must cut.*" Harder and harder she pressed, and faster and faster she moved the rope up and down against the glass. It seemed to make no difference. Whatever the rope was made of, it would not part.

'Give up, give up, *give up...*' came a quiet, insistent voice with the same timing as her movements. 'It won't work, it won't work, it won't work.'

"Yes it will," Wendy tried to say out loud, the words mumbled from behind the gag. "You're wrong!" She had no idea who she was talking to, but no longer was she going to tolerate that evil voice that always told her she had no hope. There *was* hope. She believed it. She knew it.

A second later and there was a snap like a breaking twig. The rope parted, her wrists flew apart, and Wendy collapsed on the floor. She gasped for air, the gag preventing her getting oxygen quick enough for the demands of her lungs. Shoulder muscles shouted pain as they adjusted back to a more normal position. Wendy's head swam with exhaustion, and she hardly knew what had happened. But only for a few seconds, and then the new reality dawned. Her hands were free!

As soon as she could sit up, she pulled the gag from her mouth. It had been tied tight, but Wendy managed to drag it up and over the top of her head, grimacing as it brushed against the bruises around her eyes. How good it felt to breathe properly again.

She studied her wrists, and instantly felt sick. Both wrists were a mess of torn skin. She could see some long wounds running up her arms where the glass had dug in deeply, but most of the damage was hidden beneath a gruesome pulp that gently oozed blood.

Wendy fought to keep control of herself. Panic, fear and despair were her worst enemies and she must not surrender to any of them. She had to make herself face each problem head on, and think how to overcome it.

"Right," she said. "What can I do for my wrists?" She knew she had to halt the bleeding, and protect them as best she could from further damage or infection. Obviously there were no bandages, but someone with Wendy's creativity was not going to be stopped by that. She would adapt something.

She was on the point of ripping apart one of the sheets from the bed, until she noticed again how grey and dirty it was. There had to be something better.

With her feet still tied, she pulled herself across the room, and slid open a drawer. It was where Smithers kept his shirts, all two of them.

It was beyond Wendy's strength to simply tear one apart, but she had a plentiful supply of sharp glass, and she soon cut the shirt into long strips. Carefully she wound a makeshift bandage round one wrist, swallowing hard to cope with the pain as the cloth came in contact with the bruised and bloodied skin. When it was in place, she tucked the loose end into the rest of the bandage to keep it secure, and repeated her first aid with the other wrist. When she finished, she relaxed for a second. Wendy felt a small satisfaction at having done something effective to solve a problem. Her invented bandages worked. The wrists still hurt as much as ever, but at least she wasn't in immediate danger of causing them further damage or losing more blood.

Her hands were too weak to undo the rope around her feet. But now that she was a little more in control, she kept calm. She reached for one of the larger fragments of glass, used another strip from Smithers' shirt to protect her hand from being cut, and sat patiently sawing at the rope. This time she could see what she was doing and attack one precise spot on the rope. Five minutes later her legs were free.

The rope had stopped proper circulation, and agonising cramp seized her as blood flowed back into her ankles. She had to lie as still as she could to minimise the torture. 'That was almost as bad as anything else,' she groaned inwardly as the pain finally eased.

Wendy struggled to her feet. Inside she felt a tiny glow of achievement. Getting off that bed and clear of the ropes had seemed impossible a few hours before. But she knew that was no more than a first stage. Now she was back to the same position as she'd been in yesterday, free but only to move around within a locked room with a boarded up window. She hadn't managed to escape from the room yesterday when she had that amount of free- dom. How was she going to do it now?

'"I know the plans I have for you," declares the LORD.' The words from the Bible verse came into her mind again. "I think I need to know those plans too..." Wendy said quietly in response.

She glanced over at the clock. It was after 3 p.m. There wasn't much time.

CHAPTER 13

"I don't think we're going to find this cat. We've been wandering around town for nearly three hours, and there's no sign of it anywhere." Fred didn't like having to be so negative, because he didn't want to disappoint Helen. He sensed how important it was to her to track down the injured or dead cat.

Both of them leaned against a wall. Helen was reluctant to give up, but inside she knew that Fred was right. "What can have happened to him?" she asked for probably the tenth time.

"It's possible someone picked up the body and took it away for a decent burial, or the cat was so injured it crawled off somewhere quiet to lie down and die, and we just haven't found where that is."

Helen kept silent. There were no other explanations.

"I think it's time I treated you to another sumptuous burger and Coke," Fred said more cheerily. "We need to be revived."

Helen smiled. Fred was thoughtful and generous, even though this suggestion was probably as much an act of kindness to himself as to Helen. "I'm tired too," she admitted. "Walking around hour after hour isn't easy, especially when you're just wandering, not really going anywhere." Her voice slowed. Helen was listening to her own words, and thinking.

"You know, Fred," she said a moment later, "getting weary like this is how it must have been for Wendy a couple of days ago. If she had no-one to turn to, and nowhere in particular to go, all she could do was wander round and round the town, getting more and more tired."

Fred nodded. He agreed with what Helen said, but didn't see the point of it.

"Okay," Helen went on, "let's be logical. If you had walked around for hours, and you were exhausted, what would you do?" Fred frowned. He still hadn't tuned in to Helen's line of thought. "Come on, Fred," she scolded, undaunted by the fact that Fred was three years older than her. "Think! You're the one who told me on the phone that everyone could be asking the wrong question. Remember?" Fred's face was blank. Clearly his mind was tired as well as his feet. Helen didn't wait for him to recollect. "You said the real question might not have anything to do with who Wendy would go to, but simply 'Where would she go?' And that's right. We know Wendy didn't go to any friend, because whoever has her is keeping her a prisoner. But where did she meet that person? Probably she just walked round and round until she was too tired to keep going, and then... Then what? Where would she go?"

Fred was finally beginning to see the light. "Well, if she had any money..."

"Wendy always had money!"

"Then it's likely she'd do what I've just suggested, and go to a cafe for something to eat and drink."

"Exactly!"

"Yes, good thinking. But the police will have thought of that as well, and checked with every cafe or restaurant

147

in town to see if anyone remembers serving Wendy. And, from the reports I've heard, no-one does remember her."

"Hm..." Helen's spirits sagged. For a moment she had thought she was on to something, but of course Fred was right. The police had interviewed shopkeepers, library assistants, bus drivers, taxi owners, cafe workers, postmen, milkmen, and countless others, anyone who could have had contact with Wendy.

"Come on, Helen," Fred urged, sensing her disappointment. "Let's risk the Coke and burgers at the same cafe we went to before."

Helen shrugged her shoulders. She felt so low. Fred had already started to walk off. 'God,' she prayed quietly under her breath as she stirred herself to follow, 'why can't you point me in the right direction? Why is every idea I have so useless? I just don't understand it...' With that she forced her tired feet in the direction of the cafe.

* * * * *

"You stay at home in case any news comes through. I've got to go and look for Wendy again. I can't just sit here and wait." Mr Jones was pulling on his jacket, even as he spoke.

"But where will you go?" asked his wife. "We know Wendy isn't lying injured. She's a prisoner somewhere. That means she's inside a building. How could you possibly find her?"

"I don't know," Mr Jones said. "But I can't merely watch the clock going past, hoping the phone will ring, and then being disappointed over and over again when it does and there's no news of Wendy. Look," he said, pointing at the old fashioned grandfather clock in the hallway, "it's well after 4 o'clock now. The message Wendy sent said we had only until this evening. I must go out and *do* something." His voice was agitated, his heart ever more afraid they wouldn't find Wendy until it was too late.

Mrs Jones nodded quietly. "I understand," she said, and followed her husband towards the door. She stopped him just before he left. "Take care out there," she said. "I want you to come back safely."

Lowering his eyes, Mr Jones whispered, "Are you sure?"

"Yes, I'm sure," she replied in a voice which had lost the hardness of three days' earlier. "We've a lot to put right, but I think we can do it."

"Then I'll be back, and it'll be with Wendy."

His wife smiled. She was grateful for her husband's determination, but knew it would take a miracle for his words to come true. She watched him disappear up the driveway. "God be with you," she murmured, "and give us the miracle we need."

* * * * *

"It's going to take a miracle to get out of here," Wendy said to herself. Her ability to be logical and practical was diminishing. Logic needed realistic options to consider, and how many of those did she have? She couldn't think of any way of escape.

The door was as solid as ever. It would never break, no matter how often she threw herself or anything else against it. The boards on the window were now immovable. Smithers had hammered in twice the normal number of nails to make sure that she couldn't pull any

149

of the planks free another time. 'Besides,' Wendy thought, 'even if I could, what would I do then?' She'd be killed if she jumped, and there was no-one to signal to. Smithers had persuaded Helen and her father there was no point in coming back.

Now she sat slumped against the wall. The hands on the clock across the room eased their way round the clock face mercilessly. 'How slow they move during a boring school lesson,' she thought, 'and how fast they're going now.' It was 4.15. She closed her eyes, wishing she didn't know how much time she had left.

It was obvious to her that Smithers had never intended to let her live. He had to be mad or bad, or both. He'd seemed normal - better than most people - when she'd first met him. How could he be so kind and also so cruel? Had she missed seeing something about his personality or his behaviour which should have warned her? Her mind roamed back over that meeting in the cafe, the way they had talked, and how well he had listened and been sympathetic. How easily she had been able to unburden herself to this man, knowing he accepted her for the person she was. With her Dad leaving, she'd felt so lost and unloved. But Smithers had made her believe she was important and special. He had made her feel good again. It had been easy to trust him.

'Never trust a stranger.' Now she understood why those words had been drummed into her from when she was less than five years old. But she hadn't remembered them in the cafe that day. All that had mattered was that Smithers had been helpful when she needed help.

Wendy glanced at the clock again. It was nearly 4.30. He'd be back in just over two and a half hours. "*You'll have to die. Tonight...*" he'd said. And he'd meant it.

The publicity about his name had made it certain that he'd get rid of her as soon as possible. He'd dump her body somewhere it wouldn't be found for a long time, and move on to a new area before any suspicion could fall on him.

"There must be a way out of here. There must be..." Wendy knew it. Deep inside herself she was sure. But what was it? And would she find it in time?

* * * * *

The cafe was much quieter than it had been the previous day, and Fred and Helen had no difficulty getting a seat near the window.

"Where have all the reporters gone?" Helen wondered. "I suppose it's later in the day than when we were here before."

"That's partly it," Fred said, "but it's also Saturday. There isn't such a pressure on reporters for hard news stories for the Sunday papers. They'll have written something already about Wendy's disappearance, and all they'll do now is keep in touch with the police in case there are any late developments."

"You seem to know a lot about it."

Fred smiled. "I'd like to be a journalist eventually. The school allowed me a couple of weeks of 'work experience', so I spent it with the local paper. It took some of the mystery out of reporting the news."

"Right, what can I get for you?" interrupted a voice.

"A Coke and burger for me," Fred said. "And is that alright for you too, Helen?"

There was no reply, and Fred glanced round at his companion. Helen was sitting completely still, staring straight at the young man who had come to take their order. Fred shifted in his seat, feeling uncomfortable at Helen's rudeness. "Em...I think she'd like the same..." he said.

"Okay, just give me a few minutes," came the reply and the young man moved back behind his counter.

"Helen, what on earth is wrong?" Fred asked as soon as he'd gone. Still she sat silent. "What is it? You look as white as a sheet."

Helen's eyes narrowed slightly, as if she was concentrating, trying to work something out. Finally she spoke. "Fred, I've seen that fellow before."

"Yes, of course you have. He served us when we were in this cafe yesterday."

"That's right, but I've seen him since. Do you remember the houses on the short cut home, the ones I told you were in my dream, and you said I just imagined them, that it was déjà vu or something?" Fred raised his eyebrows in acknowledgement, but said nothing. "My Dad and I took another look at them last night. We saw someone move around inside one of them, knocked on the door, and that guy answered. At the time I was so uptight I couldn't remember who he was, but this is where I'd seen him."

"I thought all those houses were boarded up."

"They are, but he said he had been allowed to stay there by himself for a few weeks."

"That seems perfectly reasonable to me."

"Yes, but he was in *that* house. There's something about it, and about him It's the house that was in my dream, and it must be more than a coincidence that the person living there also works in this cafe."

"Helen, why can't it be a coincidence? And what does

it matter anyway if the man who serves the burgers here also lives in a house you dreamed about? Try and calm your imagination down."

Nothing about Helen was going to calm down at that moment. "Fred, we agreed just a few minutes ago that Wendy might easily come somewhere like this if she was tired and alone. She could have met up with this waiter."

"But when we spoke to him yesterday about Wendy he didn't say anything about seeing her."

"Of course he wouldn't if he had something to hide."

Fred's forehead knotted in a frown. "You're a bit too suspicious, Helen."

"No I'm not," Helen went on, unwilling to back down. "There's something more... I can't quite get it clear in my mind, but isn't that guy called 'Bill'?"

"I've no idea. Why do you think that's his name?"

"I'm not sure, but I seem to remember someone called him 'Bill' when we were in here before."

Fred sat back, and took a deep breath. "It would make a big difference if he is called 'Bill'. I'd take your other thoughts a lot more seriously then."

"How can we find out?"

"Well, I'll ask him. I'll drop the question into casual conversation, and see what he says."

It was only another couple of minutes before the waiter reappeared from behind the counter, clutching a tray with two hamburgers and cartons of Coke. "Here we are, just what you ordered," came his friendly voice.

"Thanks very much," said Fred. "It seems quite a bit quieter today than when we came yesterday."

"Yes, you were here, weren't you? I thought I remembered the faces. Yes, it is quieter. I was fairly busy around lunch time, but business always goes slack by this late in the afternoon. I prefer it hectic, though. It's hard work when you have lots of customers, but it makes the time pass quickly. Right now, I'll be glad when the day is over." He smiled, and began to walk away.

"It's 'Bill' isn't it?" Fred asked politely.

The waiter stopped sharply, and looked intently at Fred, and then at Helen. "No, it's Frank, Frank Byres."

Heart pounding, Helen said, "I thought one of the customers called you 'Bill' when we were in before?"

"Sorry, young lady, you must be mistaken. Maybe the person you heard had finished his meal and he was calling for me to bring him his bill, and you misunderstood."

Helen didn't reply. "I apologise for the mistake," Fred said quickly.

"That's no problem. It doesn't matter does it...?"

Fred shrugged his shoulders, not wanting to go into any deeper explanation. Thankfully the waiter moved off.

Smithers hurried back behind his counter, glad to get away from these inquisitive young people. His hands trembled with tension, and he wondered how he'd managed to keep his voice so steady when they'd asked his name. 'If I hadn't seen the newspaper this morning and decided to use a new name, that conversation could have been disastrous,' he thought.

As soon as they'd come through the door he'd remembered exactly who Fred and Helen were from the previous day, and how they'd been looking for their friend Wendy. That hadn't troubled him, but Helen's appearance at his door accompanied by her father had been more worrying. At the time he'd congratulated himself on how well he'd got rid of them. But now she

154

was back with her friend, and trying to check his name. They were getting too close to finding out the truth.

* * * * *

Wendy sat on the edge of the bed, feeling tempted to lie down and sleep. She was sore, tired and hungry. Round and round the room she'd walked, racking her brains for a way to get out, but come up with nothing. No matter how many times she reminded herself that God had a plan, it was lost on her. So now, if she could not escape the room, at least she could escape into sleep and blot out reality for a while.

But she knew that if she did that she might waken up only in time to face death at the hands of Smithers when he returned home. To fight off the temptation to sleep, Wendy moved away from the bed, sat on the floor against the wall, and looked around. She banged the floor with her fist, more out of frustration than anger.

'I wish I could build a tunnel to get out of here...' she sighed, remembering old films of people escaping from prisoner of war camps. 'But how do you dig a tunnel through a floor made of solid oak floorboards, and especially when you're two storeys up in a building?'

Wendy slumped back, resting her head against the wall. "A tunnel..." She thought about it again, and laughed. What a stupid idea. "No it's not!" she said suddenly, her brain whirring into a new gear. "That's exactly what I need. If there's time..." Anxiously she looked across at the clock. It was 5 o'clock. She wasn't sure she could do it in two hours.

* * * * *

155

"I don't believe him," Helen said. For fifteen minutes they had analysed everything they knew about Wendy's disappearance, and nothing had shaken Helen's certainty that this waiter was a key figure. She ate the last of her burger, and drank the last mouthful of Coke. By now everyone else had left the cafe. She glanced over at the figure behind the counter. "I don't trust him and I don't believe him. I think his name *is* Bill."

Fred shook his head in mock exasperation. "I don't think I've ever met anyone quite as stubborn as you. But...," he drew his breath in deeply, and added, "I didn't like the way he looked at us and hesitated. This time you might be right."

"What can we do...? Is there any way to find out for sure what his name is?"

"I've an idea," said Fred. "Come on, let's get out of here."

"But we don't know yet what he's called..." Helen protested.

"Shh...," Fred said, putting his finger to his lips to warn Helen to keep quiet.

They stood up. "Is that you off, then?" Smithers called over.

"That's right," Fred replied, as he moved to the counter and paid for their Cokes and burgers. "Thanks for everything."

"That's fine. I'm glad you enjoyed it. Come again..."

Fred took a moment to fasten his jacket, then walked slowly back towards Helen who was waiting by the door. He seemed to take a long time. Smithers turned away to tidy up some cups and plates. That was exactly what Fred wanted to happen. He needed him to be concentrating on something other than them. He reached Helen, opened the door for both of them, and as they stepped outside called back over his shoulder, "See you another time Bill."

"Sure, cheers for now."

There was sudden silence. Smithers' words died abruptly on his lips, as he realised he'd replied to his real name.

Fred smiled at him. "Thanks Bill," he said, and promptly closed the door.

"Right, we need to get help fast," said Fred, as soon as they were out in the street. "We know who he is, but he knows we know." Fred grimaced at his own complicated sentence, but this was no time to worry about grammar. "We've got to call the police and now!"

Helen nodded furiously. "There's a phone box just a couple of streets away."

"Let's go then," urged Fred.

They turned to run. But almost immediately Helen stopped in her tracks. Something had caught her eye, something up a narrow alley alongside the cafe. "Hold on Fred!" she called.

"Helen we haven't time for anything else. We've got to get to the phone."

But Helen had already started to move very carefully up the alley. She wasn't sure what she had seen, but she had a strange feeling about what it was. It was important to go slowly and quietly. Ahead of her was a small black object, lying alongside a wall.

"What is it?" Fred asked.

"It's Abba," Helen said softly as she got closer, tears in her eyes as she realised how still he was lying.

"Is he alive?"

"I'm not sure. He must have crawled here. Maybe

that wretched man in there is his owner, and he came looking for help after the accident. How he managed to get this far, I don't know."

She bent down gently, and stroked his fur. Her touch was met by a faint "Miaoww..." A wave of relief swept over Helen.

"He might be alright," she said excitedly.

"If he is, it's a miracle," Fred said. "But I've heard stories of cats surviving terrible accidents, although never of one being hit by a bus like this one. He must be a tough cat."

"I think he is." Helen thought quickly. "Look, it doesn't take two of us to make a phone call. You go on ahead. I'll to stay here with Abba."

"I don't like leaving you here alone."

"I'm fine. That man in there isn't going to attack me in the street, because the last thing he wants is attention. And if I start screaming, he'll get plenty of that. You might be two streets away in a phone box, but even you'd hear me. You make the call. I'll look after Abba."

"Are you sure?"

"I'm sure," Helen said emphatically.

Fred knew it was pointless to argue. "Alright. Now stay near the cafe. I won't be long."

Fred took a deep breath, and started running at a speed which had won him the school athletics' championship two years in a row. Helen turned her attention to Abba.

"I wonder if you could cope with me picking you up?" she asked the cat quietly. If he had any serious injuries, she could make them worse if she lifted him. But it was too much to bear to leave him lying there on the cold pathway.

"Miaowww..." came the pitiful response.

"Listen, Abba, I'll take hold of you very gently. You let me know if it hurts." She didn't doubt that Abba would show her in very clear terms if he was in pain, either with a loud screech or the use of his sharp claws.

Helen slid one hand underneath Abba's stomach, and steadied him with the other. As slowly as she could, she lifted him carefully off the ground. There was no protest, and a moment later she had him cradled in her arms. "That's better, isn't it?" she said, trying to hold him close to keep him warm.

Helen heard the sound of the cafe door being opened. She was standing in the narrow alley, just out of sight of the entrance. Had someone gone in or come out? There was only one person who could come out... A second later she heard keys turning a lock and saw a figure hurrying away.

Smithers never noticed her. All that was on his mind was getting back to his house, killing that stupid girl Wendy, and getting clear of the town before the police could come looking for him. Now that his identity was known to these interfering young people, he had no time to waste. He would have to bring forward his timetable.

CHAPTER 14

Fred sprinted as fast as he could. If the waiter had tried to cover up the fact that he was called 'Bill', he must have known the police were looking for him. Now that he'd been found, what would he do? By uncovering him they might force him to take sudden and disastrous action. Fred had to get help immediately.

He dived and weaved his way between the few pedestrians who were still around. An elderly lady stepped out of a shop right in his path, and Fred only just skidded to a halt in time, clutching on to her as he steadied himself. "I'm sorry..." he gasped.

"Not at all, young man. It's been many years since someone as good looking as you ran into my arms," came a croaky voice.

Fred rolled his eyes, made a neat side-step, and was on his way again. At any other time he'd have enjoyed the old lady's humour, but right now a much younger girl's life depended on him getting to a phone. He put his head down, and ran for all his worth. But next second a boy with a bicycle rode up the kerb and into Fred's path, heading for the gate to his house. This time Fred couldn't stop. He careered straight into the side of the bicycle, and sent both of them crashing to the ground.

"Sorry, my fault," said the boy. "But you were

running very fast."

"It's okay, I don't care," Fred gasped, pulling himself to his feet. As he did, he winced as pain jabbed at his left knee. "Ouch...!"

"Have you hurt yourself?" asked the boy anxiously.

"I'll be alright," Fred stammered, rubbing furiously at his leg. "It'll be okay in a moment."

"I hope so," the boy replied. He pulled his bicycle up and disappeared through his gate before anything else could happen.

Fred straightened his knee slowly. That hurt badly. He tried to put his weight on the leg. It was sore, but he could stand. "I must get going," he muttered, and began to run again. Instantly he found himself back on the ground. His knee couldn't take that kind of strain, and had buckled under him. He dragged himself up, and tried another short step. There was pain but he could cope. Two, three steps followed, and then more. Running was impossible, but Fred found he could make progress providing he took it slowly.

Dragging the damaged leg, he limped along. He gritted his teeth to fight back the pain as he struggled along the road.

In the distance he saw the phone box. "Just about three hundred metres to go," Fred told himself. "You can make it." He tried to speed up, but it was difficult with one leg trailing behind the other and not always going where he wanted it to. Suddenly his toe caught a raised paving stone, and he fell forward, cracking his head on the concrete. He lay still for a few seconds, dazed and hurt. His forehead pounded. He drew his hand across his face, and found it covered in blood. He felt sick.

Fred couldn't give himself time to recover. With

willpower he didn't know he had, he pushed against a wall, and struggled back to his feet. He had to get to the phone. Minutes - even seconds - might mean life or death for Wendy.

As carefully as he could he started out again, watching closely where he was walking. His knee throbbed.

The phone was only a hundred metres away. He'd get there. He had to get there.

Each stride was agony. If he tried to bend his leg to take a normal step, he couldn't unbend it without unbearable pain. Most of the time he managed to keep the leg stiff, and that hurt less. But the effort was taking its toll on him. He sensed something trickling down his cheek, and didn't know if it was sweat or blood. Gradually nausea was mounting. Fred wanted to stop and be sick, but he daren't. The time was too precious, and if he halted he might never be able to get going again.

Fifty metres. He was nearly there. Dark mists swirled in front of his eyes, and he couldn't see properly. Fred shook his head to clear the darkness. It helped for a second or two but after another few wrenching steps the clouds were back again. Tears of pain formed in his eyes.

"I must get there. I must phone for help," he told himself. He bit his lip, and forced the sore leg to take more strides. "Keep going, keep going."

Twenty metres. Fred could see the phone box was empty. That was a relief, though he would have dragged anyone out of the box if it had been occupied. There were moments to take advantage of being large and looking fierce, but he was thankful that extra effort wouldn't be needed. Ten metres. Fred counted down the paces. Nine. Eight. Seven. Six. Five...

An overwhelming sense of relief flooded Fred's mind

as he took the last few steps. He was going to do it. One emergency call was all he had to make, and the police would come. He could only hope it would be in time to save Wendy.

Fred's hand grasped the handle of the phone box, wrenched it open, and he pulled himself inside, almost managing to ignore a final stab of protest from his knee. He lifted the phone and began to dial.

He waited for the connection. There was nothing. There was absolutely nothing. He pressed the little lever on the phone unit up and down quickly to try again. He listened. Nothing. Harder, faster, more furiously he pressed the lever. Still nothing. The phone was dead!

Fred looked down. The cable linking the handset to the main unit was torn away and dangling loose. It was useless, utterly useless. "Vandals! Please no, not a phone broken by vandals at a time like this..?"

Nausea surged over Fred, and he slumped against the phone box, only the walls holding him up.

"What am I going to do?" he asked himself. Fred knew the centre of town pretty well. There were no other call boxes in that area. Even if he did fight his way to one, it would take too long and that phone might be out of action as well. The police station... He'd have to go there.

But no sooner did he decide that than he realised he'd never make it. The futile, painful struggle of the last few hundred metres to the phone box had drained him completely. The police station was more than a mile further. He'd never reach it, not even with all the determination his six foot six frame could contain.

There was only one choice left. He'd have to get help from someone walking by.

163

Fred staggered out of the phone box, let the door close, and leaned against it. The effort hurt his leg, and he clutched it to lessen the pain. Someone was passing. "Could you help please?" Fred stammered, his words coming out uneasily because of the agony from his knee.

It was a woman with a young child. She took one look at this crouched giant with contorted face covered in blood, and snatched her daughter into her arms. "Come on, Julie," she said quickly. "Let's get away. We don't speak to strange men..." Off they ran.

Fred groaned. The woman was right - how was she to know what he really wanted? But that didn't help. The nausea swept over him with greater intensity. 'I can't faint. I mustn't faint,' he told himself, and fought to keep control. If he passed out and was taken to hospital, what would happen to Helen standing outside the cafe waiting for him to come back with the police? What would happen to Wendy, wherever she was..?

His strength was going, and Fred wasn't sure he could keep standing up much longer. He heard footsteps, and squinted to see who was coming. This time it was a man. Surely he wouldn't frighten him off? Fred raised one arm tamely to signal for him to stop, and murmured, "Please help me, I'm hurt."

The passer-by paused. It was a middle-aged man. He looked at Fred, then sneered, "You should be ashamed of yourself. You're so drunk you can't stand straight, and you're hardly eighteen." A second later he was gone.

Fred's heart sank. He'd failed. No-one was going to help. He felt his balance going, and he began to slide to the ground. His head was heavy, and he didn't seem able to keep himself from falling.

Strong arms suddenly caught hold of his shoulders.

"It's alright, I've got you," came a voice. "You'll be fine. Just sit down for a moment until you feel better."

Fred had no idea who was speaking to him, but he was in no position to argue. It was a case of either sitting down under control or falling down out of control.

"Phew, you look in a real mess," came the voice. It was a man, but not like the previous one. This one spoke gently and seemed to care. "What have you been doing to yourself?"

"I need help," Fred said as soon as he could find words.

"I can see that."

"No, not for me. I need to get help for my friend Wendy."

"What name did you say?" The voice speaking to Fred had become instantly serious and urgent. "Who do you need help for?" it pressed.

"For Wendy, Wendy Jones."

"Who are you?" the rescuer asked.

"Fred. I go to school with Wendy, and Helen and I are trying to find her."

"Right, I know Helen and I've heard of you. You're in the school play with Wendy, aren't you?"

Seated on the ground, Fred was beginning to recover, and realised this stranger knew more than could be expected. "Yes, I am in the play. How did you know that? Who are *you*?" he asked bluntly.

"Wendy's father," said Mr Jones. "Looking for Wendy just like you are."

Fred closed his eyes and breathed a short prayer of thanks. He couldn't begin to imagine what the chances were that, of all men, this one would come along at that precise moment. But there was no time to spare. "I know who's got her," Fred blurted out. "I was trying to get the police because I'm frightened something dreadful will happen to her right now, but this phone isn't working."

"Tell me what you know as fast as you can," said Mr Jones.

Fred sat as straight as he could. His head was clearing. He chose his words carefully, and in a few sentences convinced Wendy's father that she was being held by the man called 'Bill' who worked in the cafe two streets away.

Mr Jones took instant decisions. "Alright, we can't call the police, so let's get there ourselves. Helen could be in danger as well. Can you walk if I help you?"

"If you help me, I can *run*," Fred said with new determination.

Less than a minute later, Fred's arm was round Mr Jones' shoulders, easing the weight on his damaged knee, and the two were hobbling back up the street at a fast trot.

"We've got to stop this man Bill," Fred gasped.

"We'll stop him. Believe me, we'll stop him," came the growled reply.

* * * * *

Wendy lay flat on her back on top of the wardrobe, kicking at the ceiling. Getting up there shouldn't have been too difficult, only a matter of moving the chest of drawers alongside and using it as a giant step. But every effort to push such a heavy piece of furniture had sent shooting pains through Wendy, and she'd had to halt and catch her breath several times before she'd got the chest of drawers close enough. Then dragging herself from it on to the wardrobe had hurt all over again.

Finally she'd made it, and for the last twenty minutes had been making the hole for her tunnel by kicking her feet.

'I wonder if anyone has ever escaped before by making a tunnel in a ceiling?' she asked herself. There had been no possibility of breaking through the hard wood of the floor, and if, somehow, she could have prised up floorboards, the long drop into the room below could easily have killed her. But ceiling plaster was flimsy, and even in her weakened condition Wendy stood a chance of breaking it apart enough to get through.

It was thinking about escaping through a tunnel which had given her the new idea. She had remembered a time when her Dad had lifted some floorboards in an upstairs room of their house to do repairs, and he'd let her see into the hole. The floorboards rested on wooden rafters, and about eighteen inches beneath them was the ceiling of the room below. What had suddenly dawned on her now was that if Smithers' bedroom had a similar space above its ceiling, she could maybe squeeze into it, crawl along and get out elsewhere.

But once into her tunnel, a great deal depended on things she couldn't know in advance. Would the gap between ceiling and rafters above stay wide enough for the distance she had to go? Eighteen inches wasn't much to start with, and if the height of the tunnel narrowed she could get stuck. And where was she going to crawl to anyway? She needed her tunnel to take her right over the wall of the bedroom, so she could then lower herself down on to the landing outside the door. But was that possible? If the wall which separated her room from the landing went all the way up to the roof, there would be no way past. But if it reached only as high as the bedroom ceiling, her tunnel would take her over the top of it. If she could then get down safely she could escape easily by the main stairs. That was the theory. But Wendy knew the chances of success were slight. There were so many things which could go wrong.

The greatest uncertainty of all lay in a question she asked herself over and over, 'Will the ceiling hold my weight?' The plaster had thin strips of wood on its top side to strengthen it, but it was still far from substantial. If she could gouge a hole simply with her feet, how could the ceiling be strong enough to hold her up? There was one hope though. When she was up there, she'd be lying flat. By spreading herself like that, she'd distribute her weight over as broad an area as possible, like someone spread-eagling himself on thin ice to stop falling through. If that technique could work on ice, it might work also with ceilings. She had to take the chance.

Bang! Her foot crashed into the ceiling. Bang! She kicked it again. Plaster fell on her like dusty snowflakes. It had been happening since she began. She was long past caring about her appearance, but the dust irritated her eyes. As much as she could she resisted the instinct to rub, in case she scratched her eyes with grit. Bang! Another dent in the ceiling, and another shower of white dust.

Wendy rested, though on top of the wardrobe that meant little more than allowing her legs to dangle and her back muscles to relax. She had so little strength she could manage only four or five kicks between rests.

She looked at the clock. It was 5.30. "An hour and a half to go," she whispered through clenched teeth. "It might be enough."

Her efforts at creating a hole were succeeding better than she imagined, but that was only because the plaster

168

was old and therefore powdery. If that helped now, it wouldn't help later when she needed it to take her weight. But at least it gave her a better chance of beating the 7 o'clock deadline when Smithers would come home.

"I must get on..." she said, and kicked furiously at the ceiling. Bang! Another small hole appeared, and Wendy spat out the flakes of plaster which fell in her mouth. Again she kicked. Bang! Tensing her muscles, Wendy determined to give the ceiling the kick of her life. "One, two, three... Take that!" she shouted, and flung her foot up, kicking as hard as she could. Bang!! Immediately there was a loud crack. Wendy instinctively twisted her head sideways as a huge section of ceiling plaster fell. It crashed against her head, and broke in pieces on the floor. Thankfully it wasn't heavy, but Wendy knew she'd just added one more bruise to her large collection.

As the dust cleared, Wendy saw to her amazement that in one go her hard kick had created a hole big enough for her to squeeze through. Stage one of the tunnel was complete.

She sat upright, and reached to grip the edge of the hole. More plaster came away as she took hold. Wendy felt discouraged, but as she probed further back, she could feel small strips of wood that seemed to have more strength. She'd never know if they would carry her unless she tried.

Wendy tried to pull herself on to her knees. It meant squirming round awkwardly in a very small space. As she shifted, her hand slipped and she lost her balance. Instantly she grabbed on, but the wardrobe wobbled violently before steadying itself. "Oops! That was nearly a disaster," she said, bracing herself against the wall. When she felt everything was stable, she knelt properly and pushed her head through the hole, peering to see how much of a tunnel she had. What was vitally important was whether she could get over the wall of her room at the far end.

A few seconds later she pulled her head down again. It was hopeless trying to look, utterly hopeless. The boards over the window meant the bedroom generally had little light, and there was none at all reaching up into that hole. It was pitch black. She would not be able to tell if her tunnel led anywhere unless she climbed up and felt her way forward blindly.

'I can't do that...' Wendy said to herself. Some very old fears were suddenly resurfacing in her mind. 'I can't get shut in a dark place like that.' Wendy knew what was wrong. When she'd been about four years old, she'd accidentally locked herself in a cupboard under the stairs of her house. From what her mother told her later, she'd gone in to retrieve a ball, and somehow pulled the door shut behind her. In the darkness she hadn't been able to find the right place to push to get the door open again. By the time her mother heard her screams, she had been stuck in there for five or ten minutes. Even though Wendy could hardly remember the incident, ever since then she had panicked if she was in small spaces, especially if they were dark. This tunnel in the ceiling was tiny, a completely black hole. And Wendy was going to have to crawl along it in hope that there might be a way out at the other end. 'I can't do it...' she decided.

'I have plans for you... and they are not to harm you,' a reassuring voice whispered deep inside. Wendy closed her eyes and groaned. God might be behind this way of escape, but she still didn't like it. 'I can't climb up there into that darkness,' she told God.

In the distance, two storeys below, Wendy heard a key turn in a large door. It opened, then slammed shut again, followed by footsteps on the stairs.

"Smithers!" she gasped. "It can't be him yet. It's not time. He's home far too early."

She looked up at the hole, and took a deep breath. 'Alright God, I can go in there. I'm convinced!'

CHAPTER 15

Helen had been forced to take a quick decision when she saw the man she knew as 'Bill' leave the cafe. Should she follow him? Or should she wait by the cafe for Fred to return, hopefully with the police coming too?

It had taken no more than a second to make up her mind. Pulling Abba even closer so that he felt secure, she'd set off behind Smithers. She could not bear the thought of standing outside a deserted cafe while this man hurried home, perhaps to do harm to Wendy.

Keeping track of him hadn't been difficult. She'd known exactly where he would go, so she'd stayed some distance behind him and out of sight. Once away from the safety of the main street, she hadn't wanted him to see her following. He could get violent, and she wouldn't be able to do much to defend herself against a man like him.

Up a lane he'd gone, past another couple of streets, and then he'd taken the expected turn into the side street of derelict houses, and gone straight to the door where Helen and her father had spoken to him.

Now he was inside. Helen crept closer, trying not to be seen from the house. Abba purred quietly. Helen hoped that was a sign he was recovering. She stroked his head, and got an almost enthusiastic "Miaow..." in response.

"Shh..." Helen scolded, but reckoned there was little chance of Abba catching the man's attention. He was more concerned with other things. That's exactly what worried Helen. What was he doing in there? And what should she do?

"Come on Fred, I need you here," she whispered. She glanced at her watch. It was fifteen minutes now since Fred had sprinted off. Why was he so long? It should have taken him only two or three minutes to reach the phone box, another couple to make the call, and another few to get back to the cafe. When he found the cafe closed and that she was gone, surely he would guess what had happened? He knew where this house was. So what was keeping him?

A cool wind sent a chill through Helen's bones. She shivered and pulled her jacket further over her shoulders, wrapping Abba in it as well. She leaned against a wall, keeping a close eye on the door of the house. She wondered what was happening inside, and prayed a desperate prayer for Wendy's safety.

* * * * *

In his main room, Smithers frantically gathered the few possessions he needed to take with him. He'd never had to make a quick escape before. With the other girls he'd lured away he'd always been in control. Why had Wendy Jones been so awkward, right from the start? What was different about this one?

He had no time to waste on answering his own questions. He grabbed his wallet, his spare shoes, an extra sweater, and some other essentials, and laid them down outside the door ready for his getaway. There were a few more clothes he needed from his bedroom. That also meant disposing of this nuisance of a girl...

Things might not have worked out as he'd wanted, but he'd still enjoy what was to come next. He felt in his pocket for his knife. He'd need that. He grinned to himself as he thought of the terror which would be going through her mind as she lay on the bed trussed up like a turkey.

He ran up the second flight of stairs, turned the key in the lock of the bedroom door, and swung it open. His eyes peered through the gloom towards the bed. He couldn't see her.

Smithers stepped forward, wondering if the poor light was playing tricks on him. *She wasn't there!* She *had* to be there! There was no way she could have got free, and nowhere she could have gone.

His eyes adjusted to the light, and he stared around him. Strands of rope lay on the floor among chunks of debris. A moment later he saw the hole in the ceiling. Panic seized him. Had she got out? She couldn't have gone any further up, but she might have got into the next room...

He dashed through. There were no signs of her there, no more holes or fallen plaster. He checked a cupboard. Nothing. He smiled, and walked slowly back into his bedroom. "So, you're up there, buried already, eh?"

He stood still, and a second later heard a quiet shuffling above his head. He laughed. "You stupid girl, you're still stuck in this room and you can't get beyond it. You'll never escape me."

Smithers climbed on the chest of drawers and then up on to the wardrobe. He pushed his head into the hole which Wendy had made. He thought about climbing up and following her, but even leaning against the plaster told him it would never take his heavier weight. He was surprised it could hold hers.

No more than six or seven feet away, Wendy lay watching him. She'd dragged herself as far from the hole as she could, but now she was stuck in a corner and couldn't find a way out.

Smithers seemed to be looking blindly into the ceiling area, and she guessed gratefully that, while she could see him because of the dim light coming up from the bedroom, he couldn't see her in the dark corner where she was lying. Yet he'd sensed which direction she was in. Suddenly his hand flailed out, groping for her. It landed only inches from her leg. Wendy's instinct was to pull it away, but she couldn't risk it. If she curled into a ball, she would concentrate her weight on one part of the ceiling, and that might be too much. His hand stretched out again, trying to find where she was. It missed, but only just.

'If he keeps doing that, he'll catch me one time,' she reckoned. One tug on her leg would be enough to bring her crashing down through the ceiling. 'I've got to stop him.'

As silently as she could, she gathered a handful of dust. She waited until Smithers' face was turned towards her, staring into the darkness to try and see her, and then threw it hard at him. His eyes were wide open when the dust hit him. There was a howl of pain, a string of curses, and his head disappeared immediately down through the hole.

Smithers tumbled off the wardrobe, and gathered a few bruises of his own. But it was his eyes which really hurt. They stung wildly and he blinked frantically to clear the dust away. His temper erupted. He pulled out a drawer, tipped out the contents, and hurled the empty drawer at the roof. It crashed against the ceiling, making a small hole before falling back to the floor. Wendy felt the thud. She didn't know what had been thrown, but she was thankful it missed where she was lying.

The missile gave Smithers another idea.

He ran down the stairs, into his other room, and rummaged in a tall cupboard until he found his snooker cue. "This'll fix her for good," he said angrily. His patience was gone, and so was his time. He needed to kill Wendy fast so that he could get on his way.

Back up the stairs he sprinted. By now he had a fairly good idea of where Wendy was hiding. He placed himself as accurately as he could, took a firm grip of the thick end of the cue, and with a hard thrust drove the pointed tip up into the ceiling. "Take that!" he screamed, as the cue went through the plaster like a dart into butter.

Wendy felt the shaft of wood graze her arm as it shot past. It was too dark to see what it was, but she knew Smithers was stabbing the ceiling with something. It was pulled out, and a moment later she felt the cue whiz past her ear with tremendous force, stopping only when it hit the beams above her head. If he got on target, it would go straight through her.

She couldn't simply lie still and wait to die. Movement was difficult and dangerous, but Wendy slithered sideways as quickly as she dared. She had to get out of that corner. The snooker cue ripped through her floor again, just where she'd been lying a second before. If she hadn't moved, it would have got her.

The ceiling plaster under her body felt very insecure, but Wendy had no choice. She had to risk everything to get as far from Smithers as possible. There never had been much air in the roof space, and she was stirring up clouds of dust. It was hard to breathe, and Wendy gasped with the efforts she was making. But she forced herself on.

Her only chance was to get away from the bedroom. The darkness was total, so she felt her way forward with her hands. They struck something solid. A wall! 'Oh no,' Wendy groaned inside herself. 'Don't tell me I can't get across to the landing...'

There was a crash as the snooker cue was thrust into the ceiling again. This time it was a couple of feet to the side of her. Smithers' aim had become erratic. He knew she had changed position, but didn't know which direction she had gone. But the room wasn't big. He only had to keep trying to succeed eventually.

The cue was pulled out, and a tiny pinprick of light pierced the darkness through the hole it left. Wendy saw the dim shape of the wall she was against, but also a small gap half a metre along where some bricks were missing. The wall wasn't solid in that one place! She pushed on her elbows, and dragged herself in that direction.

Smithers was getting wilder with the cue, banging it through the ceiling at random. Finally the pain of aching arms overcame his anger and he rested.

Wendy couldn't afford any rests. She reached the hole. It was tiny, but also her only hope. She had to get through to the other side, out over the landing, and then further still. With Smithers in the house she couldn't escape, but she would try to put herself out of his reach. If she could lie on the ceiling over the stairwell, Smithers wouldn't be able to stretch high enough to attack her there. 'And maybe, just maybe, God will send someone to rescue me. Please God, do that...' she prayed. Deep inside, no matter how hopeless everything seemed, she still trusted.

'If I can get my shoulders through this hole, the rest of me should follow,' she calculated. One arm went through easily enough. Her head went next, but that left the other arm behind, her shoulder hard up against the bricks. That wouldn't work. She pulled her head out again, and slipped her second arm through the hole first. She buried her head between her arms, and edged forward, levering against the sides of the hole with her arms.

She thought she was making it, even if it was only an inch at a time. But just as her shoulders reached the hole, they jammed. She struggled, but couldn't go forward. She tried going back, but that didn't work either. Wendy wanted to panic. Her fears of getting trapped in the dark were rising again. "I can't do this. I can't cope..." she murmured.

'*Hope* Wendy... *Hope!*' That key word blazed across her mind again, and the panic melted. 'I'm going to do this. There's no way back, only forward,' she told herself with new determination.

She pulled her arms even tighter together in an attempt to make herself small. She lifted her feet up, and found a beam against which she could press them. 'Here goes!' she said silently. She shoved hard with her feet, and simultaneously pulled as best she could with her arms. Her body moved forward six inches. Sharp edges of bricks dug into Wendy, but her head and shoulders slid through the hole. She was out of the bedroom!

For a moment she rested and considered her strategy. As fast as she could she had to get out over the stairwell. She had walked over that landing only once, but she remembered the stairs were directly opposite the door into the bedroom. So if she went in a straight line away from the bedroom wall, she ought to get into the area Smithers couldn't reach.

She heard him stir again. Crash! The snooker cue was rammed through the ceiling somewhere behind her. He hadn't realised she had escaped from the area over the bedroom, but he would soon. She couldn't delay any longer.

Wendy wriggled her hips through the hole. She stared ahead but could see nothing. What lay over there? It was terrifying to crawl forward with no idea what might be ahead. 'There could be rats or spiders...' Wendy thought. The thud of another thrust with the snooker cue persuaded her that nothing which lay in front could be worse than what was behind.

Arms and legs spread wide, Wendy slithered on. Now she was clear completely of the hole, and lying only on the flimsy ceiling again. Inch by inch she crawled, sensing the plaster strain in places as it struggled to take her weight.

Bang! A sudden pain shot through Wendy's shin. The snooker cue had been hurled into the ceiling and crashed against her leg. Because her shin bone was so hard it had bounced off and carried on up until it hit the wood above.

Wendy choked back the instinct to scream with both pain and terror. Smithers had worked out that she wasn't above the bedroom any more, and he'd moved to the landing to carry on his murderous spearing of the ceiling. She lay totally still. He couldn't know yet where she was, and she mustn't give him any hints. One accurate thrust with that snooker cue, and she'd be dead.

* * * * *

179

"What should I do?" Helen asked herself again. She paced back and forward, tension and fear building in her. Inside that house, she was sure, was her best friend. What was happening to her? Was she even still alive?

Helen tried to shut away those terrible questions, but it was hopeless. They kept shouting in her brain.

"Where's Fred, and where are the police?" she demanded of Abba. He looked at her through glazed eyes, flashed his toothless smile, and purred quietly. She looked at her watch. Thirty minutes had passed since Fred left. "Something has gone wrong... Something must have happened to him."

She walked in front of the house, not caring now whether she was seen. "If Fred isn't coming back, then it's up to me. I can't just stand out here, and let Wendy die. I've got to try something." Helen summoned up all her courage. Directly confronting a hostile and dangerous man would put her at major risk. She lacked nothing in determination, but she was scared, very scared.

She moved quickly to the main door of the house. "Abba, I have to put you down. I might need to run when this man opens the door, and I'll never do that with you in my arms." She hoped the cat understood. Bending low, she laid Abba gently on the ground. Thankfully he stretched out his paws, and his legs took his weight. Much to Helen's surprise, he seemed to walk normally. She watched him disappear among bushes and plants alongside the house.

"Here goes!" she announced. She lifted the huge door knocker, and crashed it down as firmly as she could. Again she thumped it hard, and again. Each time a long echo reverberated up the stairs inside. Helen waited, frightened but ready for anything.

Two floors up, Smithers heard the banging on the door and stood absolutely still. Had he stayed too long? Had they tracked him to his house already? It was his turn to panic. 'Maybe I can talk my way out of this...' he reasoned quickly. 'After all, what evidence have they got against me?'

A dull rustling above his head reminded him of his biggest problem. "I've got to get rid of this stupid female. She can't be allowed to live and talk." He stabbed the ceiling with the snooker cue. "Where is she?" he shouted angrily.

Bang! The door knocker crashed down again. He wasn't going to be able to ignore it.

'If it's the police, they can't have come with a search warrant this quickly. I'll answer their questions at the door, and then send them away,' he decided.

Still holding the cue, he walked slowly down the stairs, getting his breath back after the exertion of attacking the ceiling. By the time he reached ground level, he reckoned he was calm and in control. He pulled open the door, and looked out.

"Where's Wendy?" demanded Helen.

"Get out of here. You've no business bothering me," Smithers snarled.

"Not until I've found Wendy."

"I don't know what you're talking about."

"I think you do. I think you've got her inside your house, and the police are coming right now."

That scared Smithers. He wasn't sure if Helen was bluffing or not. "Are you on your own?"

"Em... No I'm not," said Helen. She'd come with Abba. Of course she wasn't on her own.

"I don't see anyone else," Smithers said. His patience

snapped. He didn't have time for this. Pulling the door wider, he stepped outside brandishing the snooker cue. "Now, disappear, or you might find out what it's like to get a snooker cue across your head. Push off!"

Helen didn't fancy her chances against a man wielding a five foot long pole. She took to her heels, and ran back up the street.

Smithers retreated into the house, and slammed the door. He needed another few minutes to finish his business with Wendy, and then he could be off.

Two storeys higher up and in the ceiling, Wendy felt the door slam. She'd heard someone knock, and then Smithers go down the stairs. With no need to be silent for a couple of minutes, she'd crawled as fast as she could further and further out into open space. Now she reckoned she must be nearly safe. 'I must be over the stairs, and that'll be well above Smithers' reach.'

It was Wendy's last thought. With no warning at all, the plaster on which she lay suddenly gave way. She clutched desperately at a wooden beam, but grabbed nothing but thin air. There was a split second of light as she fell. Then for Wendy there was only darkness as her body crashed on to the stairs, and rolled down several steps.

Smithers heard the thud, and almost immediately guessed what had happened. He ran up, and found her body at the foot of the upper flight of stairs. Wendy lay in a crumpled heap, her legs and arms twisted, her skin white and without a trace of colour. She was dead.

"I don't need to bother with you any more," he murmured, and laughed.

Without any pity, he climbed past her body and went to his bedroom to collect a few clothes. He was tempted to stuff them into Wendy's rucksack, but stopped himself. He didn't want any evidence to associate him directly with her.

Downstairs he came, hardly giving Wendy a glance as he stepped over her. He dragged a bag of his own out of a cupboard, and pushed his clothes and other belongings into it.

Smithers looked about him. There was nothing else he had to take. But there was one last thing he needed to do. He had to destroy every shred of evidence about himself and what he'd done. He'd prepared for this a long time before in case it was required. And now it was.

He hurried to an alcove under the stairs. Stacked there were bundles of old newspapers and a dozen cardboard boxes. He pulled out a box of matches, bent low, and lit the corner of one of the papers. It burst into flame, but a second later it curiously went out. Smithers swore. Everything related to this girl Wendy went wrong. Now the paper wouldn't burn. He'd *make* it burn.

He lit it again, and then another paper, and then another. He started the fire in three places, then backed off quickly as this time the flames took hold. He watched for a moment with satisfaction. In a few minutes the walls and stairs would catch alight. By the time he was at the bus station, this building would be a raging inferno. There would be nothing left for the police to find when they came looking, not even a girl's body.

CHAPTER 16

The front door of the house opened, and Smithers stepped outside. From her vantage point across the street Helen could see he was carrying a large bag. 'He's making a dash for it,' she concluded. He couldn't be allowed to do that. They still hadn't found Wendy. Where was she? Maybe she wasn't in this derelict house after all, and he had kept her somewhere else. If he disappeared, they might never find her.

Helen crossed over, and stood right in his path, no more than a metre from him. "Where's Wendy?" she demanded. "What have you done with her?"

"Out of my way, you stupid girl. I'm in a hurry," Smithers replied.

"I'm not getting out of your way. I want to know what's happened to Wendy." Helen put her hands on her hips. She had no intention of moving.

"You want to know too much," Smithers snarled. His hand crept into his pocket and reappeared grasping an open knife. Helen felt the blood drain from her face. She had been willing to fight to stop him leaving, but she wouldn't last long against a man with a knife.

Smithers dropped his bag and pointed the knife at Helen. "I've had more than enough of you, and I'll get rid of you just like I've got rid of your friend."

He lunged forward. Helen dived to the side but felt the blade flash just an inch from her face. The next slash would probably connect. This was no time for pretending to be brave. She took to her heels. Smithers was blocking the exit from the street, so she sprinted the other way. It took her into the dead end.

There was nowhere to go. Smithers walked slowly towards her. He didn't need to hurry. He had his victim trapped. An evil grin covered his face. He was enjoying this.

"Help!" Helen screamed. "Help! Somebody help!" Her voice echoed in the evening air, but there was no reply. No-one else was around these derelict houses. Closer and closer he came. She was going to die.

'Not if I can help it,' she said to herself. Smithers raised the knife to strike. But as he did so Helen launched herself forward, ducked under his arm, and butted him hard in the stomach with her head. Smithers doubled over, gasping for air. Helen seized the moment to slip past him. Now she had to run, to run like she had never run before. Her life would depend on it.

She bolted at top speed back up the street. She didn't dare take time to look over her shoulder, but she heard footsteps and sensed that Smithers was coming after her. He could probably outrun her, but she had a good start, and knew she could make it.

She raced past a couple of houses. His feet were getting closer. She reached Smithers' house. The main street wasn't too far ahead. She would get there. Suddenly a startled black object streaked across Helen's path. There was no chance to change stride before Abba caught himself exactly between her feet and sent her sprawling to the ground. 'Abba, how could you!?' flashed through Helen's mind.

She never had time to get up. A crazed figure pounced on her, knocking her flat. Helen saw Smithers' hand with the knife raised high to strike. She twisted sideways as fast as she could and unbalanced him. He fell, and the knife dropped from his hand.

Helen grabbed for it, but Smithers was a fraction quicker and snatched it back. His other hand caught Helen's jacket, and held on. They rolled on the ground, Helen struggling furiously, fighting for her life. She jabbed a bony elbow into Smithers' stomach. That hurt him, but he didn't let go. Helen shot her fingers straight at his eyes. Smithers dodged his head to the side and her aim missed by a fraction. She punched, kicked and screamed. But this man was so much bigger and stronger.

She glimpsed the knife for a split second as Smithers drew his arm back, ready to strike a fatal blow. That fraction of time was just enough for her to grab his wrist. She held on for all she was worth. Now it was a battle of strength.

Smithers lifted himself on to his knees, so he could use more of his weight to thrust the knife towards Helen. She squirmed round on to her back, desperately pushing his arm away. But her energy was failing. She couldn't win. Inch by inch the knife got nearer.

At most Helen had seconds to live... She closed her eyes, and waited for the searing pain of the knife.

There was a sudden crash, a flurry of bodies, and the hand with the knife was wrenched away. Helen became aware of two figures rolling and fighting on the ground beside her. One was Smithers, and the other she couldn't see.

Smithers still had the knife, but Helen's rescuer had a solid grip on his arm. Now the battle of strength was much more equal. Back and forward they struggled. Helen scampered out of their path as the bodies tumbled one over the other towards her. Fists flew and legs kicked. Smithers forced himself on top for a second, but the other man shot his knee upwards and threw him off. The knife spun clear, and Helen darted forward and picked it up. Before she had to think what to do with it, the man landed a hard punch on Smithers' chin. It dazed him long enough for the man to roll Smithers on his front, get his arm up his back, and make him a prisoner.

"Phew!" the man said. "Just as well I did a bit of wrestling as a boy..." He looked up and smiled. "Hello Helen. Looks like I came just in time!"

"Mr Jones!" Helen gasped. "How did you get here?"

"He brought me..." Wendy's father answered, pointing back over Helen's shoulder. She turned and looked. Fred was hobbling towards them.

"Sorry I'm late!" he said. He was half smiling, but Helen could see he'd hurt himself and was in a lot of pain.

"I needed him to show me where to come, but when I heard you screaming I ran on ahead. Now, no more explanations for the moment. Where's Wendy?"

"I'm not sure. I think she's in this house. But *he* knows," she said, pointing at Smithers who seemed to have regained consciousness.

"Where's Wendy?" Mr Jones growled at Smithers. There was no reply. "*Where is she!?*" he shouted angrily, giving Smithers' arm an extra twist to make sure he understood the importance of an immediate answer.

"She's in there, but she's dead. You're too late, all of you," he said with a sneer.

"No, I don't believe you!" Mr Jones shouted.

"Believe what you like, but it won't change anything.

She fell, and she's dead. What would I have to gain by telling you a lie now?"

Helen began to cry. Wendy... dead? She couldn't be. Not the person she cared for so deeply. Not after so many had prayed and searched... A torrent of tears poured down her cheeks.

Silence fell on the others as the news sank in. Smithers had to be telling the truth this time. Wendy was gone... She was dead. Wendy was dead. She'd fallen...? Or he'd killed her...? What difference did it make at that moment? They would never again see her smile, hear her laugh, never listen to one of her stories. Wendy was gone forever. The two men broke down as well, deep sobs shaking their bodies. Their energy drained, the reason for urgency snatched away, they lost control and cried like little children. A friend, a daughter... the life of the girl they loved was over.

* * * * *

High up in the house, a small, frail figure stirred on the stairs. Wendy groaned, and then drew her breath in sharply as pain shot across her body and right down one leg. Her head also hurt more than ever.

"How did I get here?" she moaned softly. The last thing she remembered was dragging herself across the ceiling. Now...? She looked around. She was on her back on the staircase.

Wendy tried to move. Immediately more pain gripped her, especially in her leg, and she accepted she would have to lie where she was.

Suddenly a question terrorised her. '*Where is Smithers?*' She *had* to move, no matter the pain. 'I must get away. I've got to hide, or he'll kill me.'

But she was alone. There was no-one else there, and not a sound. But there was a smell. It seemed familiar. Smoke! Something was burning. Another minute and Wendy could hear a crackling noise from further down in the house. Flames! It took only seconds for her to work out what had happened. Smithers had abandoned her, set the house on fire, and gone.

Adrenaline surged through Wendy's hurting body. She tried to stand. Instantly pain shot through her leg, a depth of pain she could not ignore. She sank back on the stairs.

Smoke drifted upwards. She would have to do something. Swallowing hard to control the agony she felt, Wendy dragged herself off the steps and on to a small, half landing. One leg trailed uselessly behind her as she crawled along on her stomach. She peered round a corner, wondering if she could pull herself all the way down the stairs and out of the house. A deep red glow convinced her immediately she wouldn't be doing that. The fire had taken hold, and flames were licking around the flight of steps below her. There was not a chance that she could haul herself past them. Moving at all was near to impossible. Crawling through flames was sheer fantasy.

Wendy slid herself back towards the higher flight of stairs on to which she had fallen from the ceiling. She couldn't go down, so she would have to go up. Maybe, if she could get away from the flames, the fire would burn itself out before it reached her. She choked as smoke billowed up the stairway and hot air blew over her. The flames were burning brighter. The stairwell would funnel their deadly fingers of death up to her within minutes. Her idea was hopeless.

'Nothing's hopeless,' she reminded herself. 'But,' she wondered, staring at a flight of stairs that seemed to go on forever, 'how am I going to get up there?' She could hardly move, and guessed that her leg was broken. The slightest touch or bump felt like torture.

But self-pity would achieve nothing. Wendy planted her elbows firmly on the lowest step of the staircase, levered herself up, and tried to slide her body on to the step. She wanted to scream as excruciating pain gripped her side and leg, but she gritted her teeth together with a determination that made her jaw ache and masked the agony. With a final heave she made it, and sat panting for breath.

Getting air was becoming a problem, as the flames burned off oxygen and clouds of dark fumes filled the stairway. Wendy coughed violently, each cough torturing her body some more. Even ordinary breathing would have been difficult in the poor air, but Wendy was forcing herself to the limits.

She drove her mind back to the task. "One gone," she told herself, and deliberately chose not to look up and count how many more steps there were.

She pushed against the next one, desperately fought back yet more pain, and hauled her aching body up again. Her head felt it would burst with the effort, but she made it. It had been even harder this time, though. Every ounce of energy seemed to be used up, and she slumped in an anguished heap as soon as she pulled herself into position.

The red glow illuminated the stairwell, and Wendy felt the heat of the flames intensify. After all she'd been through, and all she'd tried to do, was she going to die in a fire?

Out in the street Helen, Fred and Mr Jones had fallen silent. Fred had allowed himself to slump to the ground to take the weight off his knee, Mr Jones was still holding Smithers in a vice like grip, and Helen had buried her face in a handkerchief. Each was pre-occupied with private thoughts and had nothing to say. They knew they would have to move eventually, but none of them wanted to be the first to suggest leaving.

Helen heard a rustling and crackling sound like the wind beginning to pick up. The strange thing was that she couldn't feel even a gentle breeze. She looked around, puzzled. Immediately she saw the explanation. Smoke was pouring from the front door of the house, and beginning to seep through cracks in boards over windows higher up.

"Fire!" she shouted. "He's set the house on fire!"

The others spun their heads round and stared in horror at the dense clouds of smoke. One window on the stairway had never been boarded up, and through it they could see a red glow. A moment later they heard wood splinter. Flames were taking firm hold.

Wendy's father turned away, hurting even deeper. He leaned forward, and spoke coldly into Smithers' ear. "Couldn't you have allowed me at least to collect my daughter's body? I've never met anyone so evil as you."

Smithers smiled. He cared nothing for Wendy nor for her family. Mr Jones saw his grin and pushed his face hard against the ground.

"It looks like the fire is up one floor," said Fred, watching how the smoke billowed strongest through gaps in the windows there.

"I think that's where he lived," Helen said, remembering how Smithers had come downstairs each time she'd gone to the door.

Smoke was drifting out now from every window. "The whole building will go up in flames," Fred said. "There won't be much left when this is over."

High up on the stairs Wendy knew the fire was worsening. Clouds of choking smoke made her head spin. She remembered reading that few people ever died in fires from flames, because smoke killed them first. That knowledge didn't seem at all comforting.

"God, if I'm going to die," she prayed suddenly, "I want to thank you for how you've cared for me during these last three days." The words sounded ridiculous, but Wendy meant them deeply. "I know you've been with me every moment, and you did give me hope." Tears came, and it was hard to keep talking. But Wendy had to. "God, I thought your plans were to get me out. Maybe they're not. Maybe this is all there's going to be. But even if I die here, I know now about you, and that you care. Thank you for showing me that. It's what really matters."

A cloud of sparks flew up the stairs. Wendy ducked her head, but not quite quickly enough. A tiny spark landed right on her cheek. She screamed, a loud, piercing scream of pain.

Out in the road, Mr Jones' head jerked round. "What was that?" he said quickly to the others. "I heard something. It sounded like Wendy."

Helen and Fred looked blank. "I think it's just wood cracking in the flames," Fred said.

"Are you sure?"

Fred nodded, and Mr Jones' face fell.

Helen sighed. This poor, upset man was imagining his daughter's voice. Who could blame him for hearing something he so desperately wanted to hear?

The fire ate into the walls and staircase, and another shower of sparks soared upwards. Wendy bent low, but one spark landed in her hair. She beat furiously with her hands to put it out, but not before it had burnt into her scalp. The agony was uncontrollable. She screamed again.

This time all three outside heard it. "It *is* Wendy!" said Fred in amazement, but before the words were out of his mouth Mr Jones was running towards the door.

"You can't reach her!" Fred called. "The flames are too high. You won't make it. You'll both die!"

Mr Jones hesitated for only a second. "Just sit on him," he shouted, pointing at Smithers.

"With pleasure," Fred sighed. Taking little care, he planted his considerable weight on the man who had caused all this misery.

Mr Jones found his way to the foot of the stairs easily enough because of the daylight from outside. But by the time he was six steps up the first flight it was different. Thick black clouds billowed down to meet him. He would have to feel his way forward.

He crouched low, knowing that any air there was would be beneath the smoke. After another few steps he was on his hands and knees. It was the only way to breathe.

'Where is she?' he asked himself. Wendy could be in any room of that huge house, and the near darkness of the thick smoke would make searching almost impossible. But he had to find her. Up he climbed, felt his way round the curve of a small landing, and was suddenly faced by a wall of heat. For a moment he could see a little clearer, but only because bright flames were shooting out from underneath the next set of stairs, and fire was beginning to creep up the walls beside it. 'I hope she's not any further up,' Mr Jones thought. 'That section of staircase isn't going to last long.'

Helen had said that Smithers lived up one level, so he had to check the rooms there. He pulled open a door and stumbled inside. He could see virtually nothing. "Wendy!" he shouted. "Where are you!?"

Higher up, Wendy was making a desperate attempt to drag herself on to another step of the staircase. Suddenly she heard a distant voice calling her name. It sounded like her Dad. It couldn't be...?

"Wendy!" his voice boomed again.

It *was* him! "Dad! Dad! I'm here, up the stairs."

"Hold on, I'll get to you!" Mr Jones hurried out of the room he'd been searching. Tongues of flame licked at him as he stepped through the door. He jumped back. This would be risky, but he couldn't hesitate. He dashed past the fire and took the next flight of steps two at a time.

Within seconds he was alongside his daughter. "Wendy," he said softly, bending down to her, stroking her forehead.

"Dad, I'm so glad you've come."

"I'm going to get you out, but we'd better go fast." He looked at his daughter. Her face was almost unrecognisable - bruised, swollen, and matted with blood. She was filthy, and covered in white dust. But what really concerned him was the awkward way in which she was lying. "I know you're hurt," he said. "Can you tell me where?"

"It's my side and my leg, especially my leg." Wendy grimaced as she tried to pull herself up again. "I won't be able to walk."

"That's alright. I'm going to carry you."

Mr Jones slipped one hand behind Wendy's shoulders and the other under her legs. "Let's take it slowly," he said, and eased her up into his arms. He expected a scream of pain from Wendy but there wasn't a sound. It was no wonder. She'd fainted as soon as he moved her.

Her father was almost grateful. It would help if every step he took wasn't putting her through fresh agony, though he would still have to be careful not to worsen whatever injuries she had. "But our number one concern is to get out," he said, wondering how they would ever do that.

The only way to safety was down. That was also where the fire was. 'I got up, so I can get down' he told himself with new determination.

But every second that had gone past had allowed the fire to grow. Peering into the smoke, Mr Jones could see the flames were even higher up the walls than before and beginning to creep across the ceiling. He'd have to take Wendy down through a tunnel of fire. Even worse, some of the wooden steps on the stair had begun to blacken. Carrying Wendy he weighed more than when he'd run up. Would those steps last?

Any delay could only make that problem worse. He turned his face away from the direction of the smoke momentarily, filled his lungs with air as best he could, and started downwards.

It was impossible to hurry carrying Wendy. Mr Jones concentrated on taking each step precisely. One slip, one fall, and both of them would be lost. Wendy had been lying just above the half landing, one flight of stairs up from the heart of the fire. Down that flight Mr Jones went. Half way he met the flames. He flinched. Every natural instinct told him to run away, back up the steps if necessary, anywhere to keep away from the fire. But he had to get his daughter to safety.

He edged this way and that to avoid the flames, crouching as low as he could in case his hair went on fire. In front of him now were six blackened steps, right above where Smithers had lit the fire. If he got over them safely, he still had to go across the main landing past a sheet of flames, and down another set of stairs.

He wanted to put his weight as near to the wall as he could. The edge of each tread would be a little stronger than the middle. But it was impossible. Flames licked up the walls, forcing him away. If he was to go down those steps, it would be over the centre of each one.

He took a firmer hold on Wendy. "I need extra help here," he prayed to God with simple honesty. He had to go fast to get past the flames, but he also had to go slowly in case he fell right through the staircase.

He eased his weight on to the next tread. It seemed solid enough. Now the next one. It was safe too. Another. The heat from the flames was unbearable. An oven couldn't have been hotter. Still he kept his movements steady. He managed another step.

Suddenly, blackened wood under his foot splintered. His leg plunged through the hole, and he screamed with agony as it was surrounded with flame.

* * * * *

Out in the street Fred and Helen heard the crash and the terrible scream. "It's all going wrong!" Helen blurted out. "The fire has got them."

"There's nothing we can do," said Fred quickly.

"Don't even think about it."

But Helen wasn't thinking. She was reacting. Her feet raced towards the open door of the house, and she plunged into the smoke before Fred could shout at her again. She coughed and spluttered as her lungs were choked by the fumes. There was no time to tie a handkerchief over her mouth. She had to get up those stairs and find Wendy and her father.

Peering into the darkness she started to climb. The heat and noise of the flames was overwhelming. Helen had never been near a major fire before, and would never have guessed how hot it could be. She fought off fear, and made herself go on. She found the first half landing, dragged herself round the corner, and started on the next short flight of stairs directly towards the flames. Up she went, step after step, the red glow of the fire pounding at her eyes. As she reached the main landing, the roar of flames drowned out every other sound.

Next moment she saw a silhouette lurching towards her. The figure was carrying someone else. She knew immediately it was Wendy in her father's arms.

That second Mr Jones stumbled and fell to his knees, still holding tightly on to his daughter. In an instant Helen was beside him.

"Helen," he gasped, recognising her. "It's my leg. Got trapped in the stair... dragged it out... but it's badly burned... I can't walk properly." His words came in short bursts. The smoke had gone deeply into his lungs, and he could hardly breathe. Helen glanced at his leg, and saw it was blackened from the knee down. She shuddered. How he'd staggered even a few steps she didn't know.

"Lean on me!" Helen ordered. Mr Jones had no

choice. The whole landing was going to collapse at any moment, and they had to get off it.

Helen knelt beside Mr Jones, slipped her arm under Wendy's legs, and then helped Mr Jones put his arm over her shoulders. "Up now!" she shouted, and pushed with all the strength she had. She was partly lifting two people, and Helen thought she'd never make it. Somehow they got to their feet. With Helen taking short steps, and Mr Jones almost hopping to avoid putting his burnt leg down, they moved forward.

They reached the lower stairs, grateful to get their backs to the intense heat. Helen went down one tread first, then Mr Jones limped down after her. Step by step they repeated the procedure. They managed one flight, staggered round the half landing, and struggled down the final flight.

With a surge of triumph, Helen eased them out through the door to freedom. For a moment they stood still, sucking in the glorious fresh air. A few metres away Helen saw Fred with a huge smile on his face. He was still keeping his prisoner firmly pinned down, but he was cheering and waving his arms with joy to see all three of them emerge from the building. Behind them there was a sudden huge crash. The staircase had finally collapsed. Another minute would have been too late. But they'd made it. They were out and Wendy was safe.

Helen led Mr Jones a few more agonised steps to a patch of grass, and then allowed all of them to sink to the ground. Even then, Mr Jones bit back his own pain to put Wendy down carefully. He laid her legs straight, and made sure her head was cushioned. When he was convinced she was as comfortable as he could make her, he finally slumped back, and closed his eyes. Only dimly did he hear the sound of sirens as the police, ambulance service and fire brigade all descended on the scene.

CHAPTER 17

"Hello Wendy..." a soft voice called.

Through misty eyes Wendy looked up into a pretty face surrounded by golden hair. The figure seemed to be dressed in white. "I think I'm in the next world..." Wendy murmured.

There was a warm smile. "Not quite. You nearly were, but you're still here in this life, and right now you're in hospital." Wendy tried to lift her head to look around. "No, don't do that. I think you may have a fractured skull, so I'd rather you just lay still for the moment." The words were spoken quietly, and Wendy rested. "By the way," the person in white went on, "I'm Dr Shearer, but you can call me Jean."

"Thanks Jean," Wendy said, though it felt strange to call a doctor by her first name. The doctor busied herself checking items of complicated equipment with strange flashing lights. It gave Wendy time to come to her senses.

"Can you tell me how I got here? The last I remember was lying on a stair, and the flames were getting nearer. I couldn't get away. I couldn't move..." Wendy's voice rose. She felt the fear again as her mind went back.

"Just relax. You're absolutely safe now, and you're going to be fine. Wendy, I don't know too many of the details, but I think your father got you out of the fire, and then you came here by ambulance."

"Dad! Yes, I remember Dad coming for me. I couldn't believe it. Dad!? I thought he'd given up on me, but he was there. Just when I needed him, he was there..."

Tears began to form, and Wendy got upset. Dr Shearer laid a gentle hand on her shoulder. "It's okay, Wendy. There'll be plenty of time to sort out everything later. Right now, we need to patch you up a bit. Can you tell me where you feel sore?"

"That could take quite a while," Wendy replied. "I don't think there's much of me that doesn't feel sore."

"We've got as long as it takes," said Dr Shearer reassuringly.

In the hours that followed, there were countless X-rays and tests, as Dr Shearer and others seemed to check out every part that hurt and most that didn't as well. Wendy told them as much as she could about how she'd got her injuries. She learned she was in the intensive care unit. Wires and tubes seemed to be attached to several parts of her. A nurse was by her side all the time, and when Wendy asked she explained what most of the equipment was for. Wendy couldn't take it all in, but understood they were checking that her heart was functioning properly, and putting into her what she'd missed in food and water over the last few days.

Eventually Wendy drifted off to sleep. She opened her eyes a little later to find her mother by her side. "Hello love," Mrs Jones said, tears filling her eyes as she saw Wendy awake. She was already holding her daughter's hand, and gave it a squeeze. "I want to give you a hug, but it's not really possible just now with everything that's attached to you."

"That's alright..." Wendy managed to stammer before

she began to cry as well. For several minutes they said nothing, just allowed many of their fears to dissolve in the tears. "Have you been here long?" Wendy asked eventually.

"I've been at the hospital since the police told me you were here," her mother replied. "They wouldn't let me in to see you at first because they needed to give you some urgent treatment. But the nurses were very kind, and gave me several cups of tea while I waited. And I had another visit to do."

"Another visit? Who to?"

"Your Dad."

"Dad? Where is Dad?" Wendy looked agitated. What had happened to her father?

"Wendy, he'll be okay. He hurt his leg when he was bringing you out."

"What happened?"

"I don't really know. Somehow he got his leg badly burned. Apparently they've had to do emergency treatment in the burns unit. He's been given a lot of painkillers, so it's not easy for him to talk at the moment. But they've promised me he'll be alright. Try not to worry."

The nurse who was nearby could see that Wendy was upset. "I think we'd better let her rest." She patted Wendy's hand, told her she'd be back soon, and left.

A great weight of tiredness settled on Wendy. She needed to sleep. Her eyes closed, but as soon as they did her mind slipped into a nightmare which took her back to her prison room. One moment she was being beaten by Smithers, and the next she was crawling across the ceiling staring into pitch darkness, not knowing what lay ahead. She felt herself fall, grabbing for something to hold but there was nothing... Then her mind replayed an earlier scene. She was lying on Smithers' bed, tied up, vulnerable... She felt Smither's hand. It was touching her hair... She hated it. He had to stop! She struggled to get free...

"Just stay calm, Wendy. It's okay... You're safe here. I think you've been dreaming." It was the doctor's quiet voice.

Wendy opened her eyes, and realised Dr Shearer had been stroking her head. Gradually the panic subsided. "The dream was horrible. It was so real."

"Remembering back?" Wendy nodded her eyes. "You nearly broke our heart monitor, making it work that hard," the doctor teased, and made her patient smile.

"What time is it?" Wendy asked.

"About five o'clock."

"It's meal-time, but I don't think I could eat properly yet..."

"You needn't worry, Wendy, we're not offering you any three course meals at the moment. Besides, your time clock is at the wrong end of the day. It's five in the morning."

Wendy groaned. "Five in the morning? Why are you still here?"

Dr Shearer laughed. "Don't feel guilty about it, but doctors have to be around as long as there are people like you who need to be cared for. Besides, in this place, time doesn't really exist. We hardly notice the difference between night and day."

"Don't you get tired?"

"Absolutely exhausted sometimes, if you want the truth. Now, enough about me. How are you feeling?"

"Pretty rough, I guess."

"I'm not surprised. Do you want to know what the tests have shown?

"Yes please."

"Well, so far here's your score of injuries: one broken skull; one broken leg; four broken ribs; and I lost count of all your cuts and bruises. Your lungs aren't too good either because of the smoke you inhaled." She paused, before adding, "My guess from looking at the X-rays is that you've had two of your ribs broken for a couple of days, and then the other two were hurt along with your leg and head when you fell through the roof. If I'm right, I'm amazed at all you did with broken ribs."

Wendy smiled, then closed her eyes briefly, trying to take in what those injuries meant. "Will I get well, Jean?"

"Of course you will," the doctor replied. "We fix almost anything around here. You've got the 'A team' working on you." They both laughed.

"How is my Dad?" Wendy asked.

"He's in the burns unit, isn't he? If you can wait for just a few minutes, I'll make a phone call and find out how he's doing. Would that interest you?"

"That would be great. Thanks."

"First class service for any friend of mine," Dr Shearer laughed, and disappeared.

Within ten minutes she was back. She smiled reassuringly at Wendy. "Do you want the good news or bad news first?"

"I think it had better be the bad news."

"Okay. Your Dad has got some nasty burns on his lower leg. His foot is alright, because his shoe seems to have protected him. But from the knee down to the ankle it's a bit of a mess, and he's in quite a lot of pain though they're dealing with that right now."

"The good news?"

"The good news is that eventually he'll be okay and so will his leg. He's not going to lose any of his vital functions, so he'll be able to walk quite normally. They can't say yet just how much work they'll have to do, but the way they treat burns these days is very effective. The skin is damaged and will never look quite right again, but I don't suppose your Dad ever thought his ankles were his best part anyway."

"No," Wendy smiled. "Thanks Jean. I'm glad it's not worse."

"He'll be fine. You can have a competition with him to see who gets home first."

Wendy's face fell, and Dr Shearer realised she must have said the wrong thing. Both stayed silent. "He doesn't live at home any more," Wendy explained finally. "In a way that's what caused all the problems, though my way of dealing with the situation didn't help." Dr Shearer listened as Wendy told her the story.

"Family life isn't always easy, is it?" said Dr Shearer after a little time, bringing the conversation to an end in case Wendy weakened herself. "But don't lie there thinking everything is bad. There are a lot of good things in your life too. For one thing your Dad must really care for you to have come into that fire to get you. And for another thing, you're alive. From the way you looked when they brought you in, and from what you've told me since, that seems pretty remarkable. I think someone's watching over you."

Wendy nodded slowly. "Yes," she said. "I think someone is."

* * * * *

During the following day Wendy got gradually stronger. Various doctors and nurses busied themselves around her. When they'd finished Wendy felt she was covered from head to foot in bandages and plaster.

Her mother made short visits, and brought her more news of her father who seemed to be doing as well as he could. She was able to tell Wendy that Fred was in hospital too, suffering from concussion, and a fractured knee which had been made worse by him attempting to run with it.

But much was still a blur to Wendy. She heard snippets of news but couldn't make sense of them. It was like having the pieces for a jigsaw but not knowing how they all fitted together. At other times, the terror and pain of Smithers' bedroom pushed its way back to the fore-front of her mind. She would sweat and tremble, but usually the nurse would notice, distract her thinking and cool down her face with a cloth.

At one point she was judged fit enough for a police-woman to be allowed to see her. Wendy was surprised to find the policewoman wasn't wearing a uniform. She asked some questions which Wendy couldn't make her-self answer, but the policewoman assured her it didn't matter for the moment and that it was much more important that she simply got better.

Later that night her doctor friend Jean was back on duty. Wendy was pleased to see her, and she was delighted with the progress Wendy was making.

For a time there was a flurry of activity as new patients arrived. Finally it subsided, and Dr Shearer sat down beside Wendy. This doctor really seemed to care, not just about putting Wendy right physically but about how she was feeling deep inside herself. Slowly, Wendy found she could talk about what it had been like to be shut up in that room, how frightened she had been of Smithers, and a little of what he had done to her. It hurt, and there were still some things which were too difficult to speak about.

"Thanks for listening, Jean," she said when their conversation came to an end. "It really helped to tell someone. You don't mind me talking, do you?"

"Of course not. What you shared really matters, because you really matter. Never forget that."

Wendy rested, grateful not to have to carry the burden of what had happened all by herself.

* * * * *

It was the next day. Helen and her mother walked through the automatic doors into the entrance hall of the large hospital. "Well, which one are you going to visit first?" asked her mother, with a slight chuckle in her voice. "I phoned earlier, and Wendy has been moved out of the intensive care unit. So you can take your choice from seeing her in the high supervision ward, Fred in the orthopaedics ward, or Mr Jones in the burns unit. Perhaps you'd like to sit and hold Fred's hand...?"

Helen frowned at her mother, not appreciating being teased. She liked Fred, but didn't want her mother creating a romance for her, especially since she suspected he was more interested in Wendy. "I've been in to visit Fred already, and you can go to see Mr Jones," she said firmly. I'm off to see Wendy."

Apart from Mrs Jones no-one had been allowed to visit Wendy in the intensive care ward. But now her condition was stable she'd been moved to a ward where she would still get close attention but without all the sophisticated equipment. And some visiting was allowed.

Helen had hardly had a moment to herself the previous day. Inspector Wilson had talked to her for a long time, and then she'd found herself hounded by reporters from TV, radio and newspapers. The dramatic rescue of Wendy was headline news, and with all the others in hospital Helen was the only key figure they could interview. By the time the final reporter was finished, Helen was exhausted and had decided that being famous was not all fun.

But now her energy was back. She bounded up the stairs of the hospital, excitement making her run along the corridor. She slowed to a halt as she reached the ward, and got directions from a nurse. Wendy had been put in a room by herself. Helen pushed open the door slowly and crept in. A figure swathed in bandages lay still on the bed.

She tiptoed her way forward, but wasn't quiet enough. "Who's that?" called Wendy's voice. She knew she wasn't allowed to look up quickly.

"Just an old friend..."

"Helen!" Wendy shouted enthusiastically and tried to sit up. "Ouch!" she said immediately, feeling some of her injuries protest at the movement. "That was sore, but worth it. I'm so glad to see you."

"And I'm so glad to see you in one piece, even if you do look like you've been wrapped up ready to go in the post." Both of them laughed, far longer and harder than Helen's humour deserved.

Then they talked. Words poured out faster than bullets from a machine gun. There were so many details neither of them really understood.

"I still don't know how you found me..." said Wendy.

"You sent a message, and the cat brought it right to my feet."

"But that's impossible. I realised the message, or part of it at least, must have got out. But the cat fell. He was killed. He must have been, falling from that height."

"No, he wasn't. And I think I know how. I went back to have a look, and there's a tree at one side of the building. By the way," she interrupted herself, "you should see the building now. Or, rather, you can't see the building now. It was completely burnt down. You'd never have survived if you'd stayed inside. Anyway, there's a tree to one side. When we found the cat he was scratched and there was a twig sticking into him. I think his fall must have been broken by the tree and that's how he survived."

On they went, filling in more of the gaps. Wendy explained how she'd got herself free from the ropes, and climbed up into the ceiling. Helen told her how she and Fred had gone back to the cafe, and found out Smithers' real name. "Then," she went on, "after Fred went to phone for help, I had to follow Smithers back to his house and wait. It was terrible. I didn't know what was going on inside."

"What was going on was nearly the end of me..." Wendy said, and told Helen about hiding in the ceiling while Smithers tried to pin her to the rafters.

"I wish I'd tried to distract him earlier," Helen sighed.

"Then I fell. What I still don't understand is why Smithers left me on the stairs when he was so desperate to kill me."

"Inspector Wilson told me the answer to that. Smithers

was sure you were already dead. The police think the white roofing plaster had made your skin so pale, it fooled him."

"It's a drastic form of make-up," Wendy said quietly.

"When he finally came out of his house, I thought he was going to kill *me*," Helen went on. She described her fight with Smithers, and how he'd come at her with a knife in the dead-end street.

"That's my part in the school play," Wendy laughed. "You can be my stand-in if I don't get well quick enough!"

"Not a chance," Helen said firmly. "That bit of drama was enough to last me a long time. Anyway, it was your Dad who saved me. He got there just in time. It seems Fred's knee got worse and worse as they tried to get back to the cafe, and your Dad almost had to carry him some of the way. Can you imagine that? No wonder it took them so long, but he got there, and then you should have seen him fight!"

They were in the middle of talking through the final stages of the story, when the door of her room was pushed open.

"Mum!" Wendy said.

Mrs Jones moved over to the bed, and kissed Wendy gently on the cheek. "How are you today?" she asked.

"Much better."

Helen got up to leave. She didn't want to be in the way when Wendy was talking to her mother. Wendy looked disappointed.

Mrs Jones spoke before Wendy could protest. "Helen, why don't you pay a quick visit to Fred, and then come back and have a final word with Wendy before you leave the hospital? Actually, I met your Mum and she was on her way to see Fred too."

That puzzled Helen, for she knew her mother was visiting Mr Jones. But Mrs Jones' idea sounded good, and she readily agreed. As soon as she stepped outside Wendy's room, she understood why her mother had moved on to her next visit. Propped up in a wheelchair, and ready to see his daughter, was Mr Jones. "Ssh..." he said, gesturing for Helen not to spoil the surprise.

Helen smiled, and whispered, "How are you?"

"Still sore, and not sure I'll ever win the 100 metres race at the Olympics, but otherwise fine," he whispered back.

"Good. I'll see you later," said Helen, disappearing down the corridor as Mrs Jones came to wheel her husband in. Just as she reached the far end, Helen heard a delighted shriek of '*Dad!*' in Wendy's unmistakable tones. 'I should have guessed her voice would be the first part of her to heal,' Helen thought, laughing to herself.

* * * * *

Wendy's parents sat side by side as they talked with her. At times all three were lost on which part of the story to try and get straight next. But it didn't matter. There would be other moments for that. As the conversation went on, Wendy could not understand the way her parents kept smiling at each other so fondly. A minute later she noticed that they were holding hands, their fingers intertwined. Their marriage was splitting up but they were being embarrassingly romantic.

She didn't have long to puzzle about it. "As soon as I get out of here, I'm coming home," her Dad said. "I've been so wrong in many of the things I've done. I can't undo those things, but I can say sorry to both of you, sorry to God, and get my life straight again."

"Sorry to *God?*" Wendy echoed questioningly.

"Yes, that's right." Mr Jones looked over at his wife, who nodded encouragement to him. "We've both learned an awful lot in these last few days." He smiled. "You'd have been surprised to see us down on our knees praying."

"Praying?"

"That's right," her Mum said. "And it was your Dad's idea. It seemed to make all the difference, and we're not going to stop doing it now. I hope you can cope."

Wendy took a deep breath. If her parents could tell her of their new faith, she could tell them her experience of God. "You're not going to believe this, but I started praying too. God seemed to be right beside me in that locked room. Somehow I knew he was really there." She took a moment to remember back, then added, "I asked him to take charge of my life."

"That's what we've been asking as well," her Mum burst out. We could be together in this as a family!" The last word lodged at the front of her thoughts. "A family - that would be so good."

A moment later their eyes were closed, and Mr Jones was doing his best to say a prayer. It was harder than ever to pray, partly because he was in a hospital ward, but also because there were no words which could properly express how grateful he felt for the new start they had been given. Yet deep down he meant the few stumbling words that came out, and so did the others. When he finally said 'Amen' their hearts were full.

Precisely on cue, the door barged open and there was

Fred, wheeled in by Helen and her mother. "He insisted on seeing Wendy..." Mrs Shaw shrugged.

"If you hadn't wheeled me, I'd have got up and walked again," said Fred. "Hi pal!" he said to Wendy as he was parked beside the bed. "Are they looking after you here, or do you need me to sort them out?"

Wendy laughed. "They're doing okay."

"Are you going to mend in time?"

"In time?" Wendy quizzed.

"In time for the school play, of course. We can't do it without you."

"We'll see," said Mrs Jones protectively. "She's going to take a long time to be really fit."

"You could always use Helen instead," Wendy said. "I gather she's been getting practice at being chased by a man with a knife."

Fred pushed himself a little closer, and smiled at Wendy. A second later she felt her fingers being held gently. "It wouldn't be the same. I couldn't chase anyone else," he said quietly.

* * * * *

Two weeks later, Mrs Jones turned the car into the driveway, pulled it to a halt in front of the house, and turned to look at Wendy sitting beside her. "Home at last! How do you feel?"

"Great! Hospital was okay, but this is where I've wanted to be." She pushed her car door open, and Mrs Jones hurried round to help her out. It still wasn't easy for Wendy to walk and her mother wanted to make sure she didn't fall over on her first day home and get taken back to hospital.

"Where's Dad?" Wendy asked as they made their way through the front door.

"I'm here," said Mr Jones emerging from one of the back rooms. "I was just seeing to something." He gave his daughter a gentle hug, making sure not to damage fragile ribs. "With you at home as well, now we can be complete."

"You mean, 'you, Mum, me... and God'?" said Wendy.

Her Dad laughed at his daughter's attempt to sound spiritual. "Something like that. Although, actually, that's not quite right. We've asked someone else to come and live with us. He's through the back there. Helen brought him over and she's talking to him just now."

Wendy was puzzled, and began to feel uneasy. She didn't want someone else coming to stay with them, spoiling the new closeness with her parents that had become so special to her.

Her father was ushering her through to the back room. She didn't have any choice. Reluctantly, she took careful steps along the hallway and through the door her father was holding open. There was Helen, and perched up in front of her was a dark face that immediately parted to show a large toothless grin.

"Gappy!" Wendy shouted, hurrying over towards the cat.

"Gappy?" said Helen. "He's Abba!" She laughed, realising that they had never used the cat's name any time they had talked about him.

"He's not Abba, he's Gappy!" Wendy insisted. "Whatever you've called him, I knew him as Gappy first." She wrapped her arms round the cat, eased him off Helen's knee, and held him close. "Where did you find him? And when?"

"Hmm," Mr Jones sighed. "I guess we've kept his presence a bit of a secret. The truth is that he's been living here for most of the time you've been in hospital. Helen went back to look at the burned-out building, and the cat found her. He must have stayed in that area, and then come out when he saw a familiar face. Helen couldn't leave him there, and because he was important in your escape she thought you might like to have him."

"Helen, thank you," said Wendy, overcome with excitement. "You're a good friend." She turned to her mother. "We can really keep him?"

"It's alright with me. Any cat that helps save my daughter's life is welcome in this house! And we've checked with the police. As far as they know, no-one owned the cat. Smithers must have fed him occasionally, but he's gone for many, many years. There's no-one else. They were grateful we could give the cat a home."

Wendy hugged Gappy. "That's wonderful!" she said. "This is the best welcome home present I could have had." She looked over at her parents. Her Dad's arm was around her Mum's waist, and her arm round his. "Okay," Wendy said, "having my Mum and Dad together again is the best. But Gappy is a good second!"

Other fiction titles for you to enjoy.

Published by Christian Focus Publications.

Classic

Fiction

Christie's Old Organ

By O F Walton

Christie knows what it is like to be homeless and on the streets - that's why he is overjoyed to be given a roof over his head by Old Treffy, the Organ Grinder. But Treffy is old and sick and Christie is worried about him. All that Treffy wants is to have peace in his heart and a home of his own. That is what Christie wants too. Christie hears about how Heaven is like Home Sweet Home. Everytime he plays it on Treffy's barrel organ he wonders if he and Treffy can find their way to God's special home. Find out how God uses Christie and the old Barrel organ and lots of friends along the way to bring Treffy and Christie to their own Home Sweet Home.

Classic Fiction

A Peep Behind The Scenes

By O F Walton

Rosalie and her mother are tired of living a life with no home, no security and precious little hope. But Rosalie's father runs a travelling theatre company and the whole family is forced to travel from one town to the next year in year out. Rosalie's father has no objections but Rosalie's mother remembers a better life, before she was married when she had parents who loved her and a sister to play with. Through her memories Rosalie is introduced to the family she never knew she had. Rosalie and her mother are also introduced to somebody else - The Good Shepherd. They hear for the first time about the God who loves them and wants to rescue them and take them to his own home in Heaven. Rosalie rejoices to hear about a real home in Heaven that is waiting for her but will she finally find this other home that she has heard about - or is it too late? Will God help her find her family as he helped her find him? Of course he will!

Classic

Fiction

The Basket of Flowers

By Christoph Von Schmid

Mary grows up sheltered and secure in a beautiful cottage with a loving father. She learns lessons about humility, purity and forgiveness under her father's watchful gaze. However, it doesn't last. Even though she loves God and obeys him this does not protect her ultimately from the envy and hatred of others. Mary is given a generous gift of a new dress from her friend Amelia, the daughter of the local landowner. This incites envy from Juliette, Amelia's maid who had wanted the dress for herself. When Amelia's mother's ring goes missing Juliette decides to pass the blame onto Mary. Both Mary and her father are imprisoned for the crime and eventually exciled from their home. Mary learns to trust in God completely as difficulty follows after difficulty. Even when she doubts if she will ever clear her name she turns back to God who is a constant source of comfort to her. Who did steal the ring in the end? That is the final unexpected twist in the tale which makes this book a really good read.

Look out for our

New Fiction Titles

Twice Freed
Patricia St. John

Onesimus is a slave in Philemon's household. All he has ever wanted is to live his life in freedom. He wants nothing to do with Jesus Christ or, the man, Paul, who preaches about him.

Onesimus plans to make his escape one day. He gets his chance in the middle of an earth quake. After he manages to steal some money from his master Onesimus sets of for a life of freedom. Along the way he meets friends and enemies and fights for his life as a gladiator in the Roman arena. Will Onesimus escape? Will he one day find his way back to Eireene the beautiful young merchant's daughter? Find out what happens and if Onesimus realises the meaning of true freedom!

ISBN: 185792-489-4

Look out for our

New Fiction Titles

Something to Shout About
Sheila Jacobs.

Jane is back in her old home town of Gipley but things are not the same as they were, in more ways than one. Heather's mum has got a slimy new boyfriend, Heron introduces everybody to her very good looking brother, Woody and it seems as though Heather's church is now going to get closed down. Woody persuades Jane and Heather to spear head a 'Save our Church' campaign. Soon the girls are up to their necks in banners, slogans and campaign strategies. However nobody has thought to ask God what he thinks of the whole situation. Eventually Jane learns a valuable lesson about prayer and seeking God's will in every situation.

ISBN: 1-85792-488-6

Look out for our

New Fiction Titles

Martin's Last Chance
Heidi Schmidt.

Rebekka and Martin live in Germany. They are firm friends and hang out everywhere together. Rebekka has a sweet tooth and a tendency towards shop lifting. Martin is a Christian and wants to introduce Rebekka to the God who loves her - he also wants her to stop stealing sweets from the corner shop! Martin however has a rare heart and lung disorder and is waiting for his last chance to get a transplant.

See how Martin trusts God throughout his illness. Find out how he and Rebekka cope with the school bullies and how Rebekka finds out for herself who God is and what he is all about.

ISBN: 1-85792-425-8

TRAIL BLAZERS

This is real life made as exciting as fiction! Anyone of these trailblazer titles will take you into a world that you have never dreamed of. Have you ever wondered what it would it be like to be a hero or heroine? What would it be like to really stand out for your convictions? Meet William Wilberforce who fought to bring freedom to millions of slaves. Richard Wurmbrand survived imprisonment and torture. Corrie Ten Boom rescued many Jews from the Nazis by hiding them in a secret room! Amazing people with amazing stories!

This is a series worth collecting!

CHRISTIAN FOCUS

Good books with the real message of hope!

Christian Focus Publications publishes biblically-accurate books for adults and children.

If you are looking for quality bible teaching for children then we have a wide and excellent range of bible story books - from board books to teenage fiction, we have it covered.

You can also try our new Bible teaching Syllabus for 3-9 year olds and teaching materials for pre-school children.

These children's books are bright, fun and full of biblical truth, an ideal way to help children discover Jesus Christ for themselves. Our aim is to help children find out about God and get them enthusiastic about reading the Bible, now and later in their life.

**Find us at our web page:
www.christianfocus.com**